Once again Steve Dalt was faced with the task of finding a new planet to call home. His acquaintances on Derby had been eyeing him strangely of late and it was time to move. Dalt had not aged a day in the decades they had known him. Possessed of a second but alien consciousness that was active down to the cellular level, his body renewed and repaired itself on a minute-to-minute basis.

So, at the ripe young age of 218, he migrated to Tolive, the notorious world of the neo-anarchists . . .

Berkley books by F. Paul Wilson

HEALER
THE KEEP

F. Paul Wilson

HEALER

BERKLEY BOOKS, NEW YORK

To Mary

PROLOGUE

Dr. Rond watched the surging crowd outside the hospital gates. Waving, pushing, shoving, shouting people, all trying to get into the hospital. Most of them wanted just a glimpse of The Healer but a good number wanted to touch him—or better yet, be touched by him—in hopes of being cured of one malady or another. Often they were cured. Dr. Rond shook his head in wonder at the placebo power that surrounded this man.

The extra security forces necessitated by the presence of The Healer within the hospital had initially given him second thoughts about the wisdom of inviting him here. But after seeing the wonders he had achieved with the resident victims of the horrors, he congratulated himself on the decision.

He turned his back to the window and looked across the room. The Healer was at work on another horrors victim, a middle-aged male this time.

Quite a figure, this man called The Healer. A flame-stone slung at his throat, yellow-gold skin on his left hand, and atop the clutter of his dark brown hair, a patch of snowy white.

He was sitting opposite the patient, hands resting on the man's knees, head bowed as if dozing. Sweat broke out on his brow and his eyelids twitched. The tableau persisted for some minutes, then was shattered by a groan from the patient as he suddenly lurched to his feet and looked around.

"Wh . . . where am I?"

Attendants glided from the corners, and with gentle support and reassuring words led him away. Dr. Rond watched him go. More-conventional modes of therapy could now be used to rehabilitate him completely. But The Healer had made the all-important initial breakthrough: A man who had been totally unable to react to external stimuli for seven standard years was now asking where he was.

Dr. Rond shook his head again, this time in admiration, and returned his attention to The Healer, who was slumped in his chair.

What a burden to have such a gift, he thought. *It seems to be taking its toll.* On a number of occasions he had noticed The Healer's habit of muttering to himself. Perhaps The Healer was himself psychologically deranged. Perhaps there lay the key to his unique talent. Between patients he seemed to withdraw completely, muttering now and again and gazing at a fixed point in space. At this moment, The Healer's thoughts seemed to be hundreds of years and hundreds of millions of kilometers away.

PART ONE:

Heal Thyself

YEAR 36

The Healer was a striking, extraordinary man whose identity was possibly the best-kept secret in human history. To this date, after hundreds of thousands of research hours by countless scholars, it remains an enigma. There can be no doubt that he led a double existence much like that of the romantic fictional heroes of yore. Considering the hysterical adulation that came to focus on him, an alter ego was an absolute necessity if he was to have any privacy at all.

For some inexplicable reason, however, the concept of a double identity became subject to mythification and evolved into one of the prime canons of The Healer liturgy: that this man had two minds, two distinct areas of consciousness, and was thereby able to perform his miraculous cures.

This, of course, is preposterous.

from *The Healer: Man & Myth*

by Emmerz Fent

I

THE ORBITAL SURVEY had indicated this clearing as the probable site of the crash, but long-range observation had turned up no signs of wreckage. Steven Dalt was doing no better at close range. Something had landed here with tremendous impact not too long ago: There was a deep furrow, a few of the trees were charred, and the grass had not yet been able to fully cover the earth-scar. So far, so good. But where was the wreckage? He had made a careful search of the trees around the clearing and there was nothing of interest there. It was obvious now that there would be no quick, easy solution to the problem, as he had originally hoped, so he started the half-kilometer trek back to his concealed shuttle-craft.

Topping a leafy rise, he heard a shout off to his left and turned to see a small party of mounted colonists, Tependians by their garb. The oddity of the sight struck him. They were well inside the Duchy of Bendelema, and that shouldn't be: Bendelema and Tependia had been at war for generations. Dalt shrugged and started walking again. He'd been away for years and it was very possible that something could have happened in that time to soften relations between the two duchies. Change was the rule on a splinter world.

One of the colonists pointed an unwieldy apparatus at

Dalt and something went *thip* past his head. Dalt went into a crouch and ran to his right. There had been at least one change since his departure: Someone had reinvented the crossbow.

The hooves of the Tependian mounts thudded in pursuit as he raced down the slope into a dank, twilit grotto, and Dalt redoubled his speed as he realized how simple it would be for his pursuers to surround and trap him in this sunken area. He had to gain the high ground on the other side before he was encircled. Halfway up the far slope, he was halted by the sound of hooves ahead of him. They had succeeded in cutting him off.

Dalt turned and made his way carefully down the slope. If he could just keep out of sight, they might think he had escaped the ring they had thrown around the grotto. Then, when it got dark—

A bolt smashed against a stone by his foot. "There he is!" someone cried, and Dalt was on the run again.

He began to weigh the situation in his mind. If he kept on running, they were bound to keep on shooting at him, and one of them just might put a bolt through him. If he stopped running, he might have a chance. They might let him off with his life. Then he remembered that he was dressed in serf's clothing and serfs who ran from anyone in uniform were usually put to the sword. Dalt kept running.

Another bolt flashed by, this one ripping some bark off a nearby tree. They were closing in—they were obviously experienced at this sort of work—and it wouldn't be long before Dalt was trapped at the lowest point of the grotto, with nowhere else to go.

Then he saw the cave mouth, a wide, low arch of darkness just above him on the slope. It was about a meter and a half high at its central point. With a shower of crossbow bolts raining around him, Dalt quickly ducked inside.

It wasn't much of a cave. In the dark and dampness Dalt soon found that it rapidly narrowed to a tunnel too slender for his shoulders to pass. There was nothing else for him to do but stay as far back as possible and hope for the best . . . which wasn't much no matter how he looked at it. If his pursuers didn't feel like coming in to drag him out, they could just sit back and fill the cave with bolts. Sooner or later one would have to strike him. Dalt peered out the opening to see which it would be.

But his five pursuers were doing nothing. They sat astride their mounts and stared dumbly at the cave mouth. One of the party unstrung his crossbow and began to strap it to his back. Dalt had no time to wonder at their behavior, for in that instant he realized he had made a fatal error. He was in a cave on Kwashi, and there was hardly a cave on Kwashi that didn't house a colony of alarets.

He jumped into a crouch and sprinted for the outside. He'd gladly take his chances against crossbows rather than alarets any day. But a warm furry oval fell from the cave ceiling and landed on his head as he began to move. As his ears roared and his vision turned orange and green and yellow, Steven Dalt screamed in agony and fell to the cave floor.

Hearing that scream, the five Tependian scouts shook their heads and turned and rode away.

It was dark when he awoke and he was cold and alone . . . and alive. That last part surprised him when he remembered his situation, and he lost no time in crawling out of the cave and into the clean air under the open stars. Hesitantly, he reached up and peeled from his scalp the shrunken, desiccated remains of one dead alaret. He marveled at the thing in his hand. Nowhere in the history of Kwashi, neither in the records of its long-extinct native race nor in the memory of anyone in its degenerated splinter colony, had there ever been mention of someone surviving the attack of an alaret.

The original splinter colonists had found artifacts of an ancient native race soon after their arrival. The culture had reached preindustrial levels before it was unaccountably wiped out; a natural cataclysm of some sort was given to blame. But among the artifacts were found some samples of symbolic writing, and one of these samples—evidently aimed at the children of the race—strongly warned against entering any cave. It seemed that a creature described as the *killing-thing-on-the-ceilings-of-caves* would attack anything that entered. The writing warned: "Of every thousand struck down, nine hundred and ninety-nine will die."

William Alaret, a settler with some zoological training, had heard the translation and decided to find out just what it was all about. He went into the first cave he could find and emerged seconds later, screaming and clawing at the furry little thing on his head. He became the first of many fatalities attributed to the *killing-thing-on-the-ceilings-of-caves*, which were named "alarets" in his honor.

Dalt threw the alaret husk aside, got his bearings, and headed for his hidden shuttlecraft. He anticipated little trouble this time. No scouting party, if any were abroad at this hour, would be likely to spot him, and Kwashi had few large carnivores.

The ship was as he had left it. He lifted slowly to fifty thousand meters and then cut in the orbital thrust. That was when he first heard the voice.

("Hello, Steve.")

If it hadn't been for the G-forces against him at that moment, Dalt would have leaped out of his chair in surprise.

("This pressure is quite uncomfortable, isn't it?") the voice said, and Dalt realized that it was coming from inside his head. The thrust automatically cut off as orbit was reached and his stomach gave its familiar free-fall lurch.

("Ah! This is much better.")

"What's going on?" Dalt cried aloud as he glanced frantically about. "Is this someone's idea of a joke?"

("No joke, Steve. I'm what's left of the alaret that landed on your head back in that cave. You're quite lucky, you know. Mutual death is a sure result—most of the time, at least—whenever a creature of high-level intelligence is a target for pairing.")

I'm going mad! Dalt thought.

("No, you're not, at least not yet. But it is a possibility if you don't sit back and relax and accept what's happened to you.")

Dalt leaned back and rested his eyes on the growing metal cone that was the Star Ways Corporation mothership, on the forward viewer. The glowing signal on the console indicated that the bigger ship had him in traction and was reeling him in.

"Okay, then. Just what *has* happened to me?" He felt a little ridiculous speaking out loud in an empty cabin.

("Well, to put it in a nutshell: You've got yourself a roommate, Steve. From now on, you and I will be sharing your body.")

"In other words, I've been invaded!"

("That's a loaded term, Steve, and not quite accurate. I'm not really taking anything from you except some of your privacy, and that shouldn't really matter since the two of us will be so intimately associated.")

"And just what gives you the right to invade my mind?" Dalt asked quickly, then added: *"—and* my privacy?"

("Nothing gives me the right to do so, but there are extenuating circumstances. You see, a few hours ago I was a furry, lichen-eating cave slug with no intelligence to speak of—")

"For a slug you have a pretty good command of the language!" Dalt interrupted.

("No better and no worse than yours, for I derive whatever intelligence I have from you. You see, we alarets, as you call us, invade the nervous system of any creature of sufficient size that comes near enough. It's an instinct with us. If the creature is a dog, then we wind up with the intelligence of a dog—that *particular* dog. If it's a human and if he survives, as you have done, the invading alaret finds himself possessing a very high degree of intelligence.")

"You used the word 'invade' yourself just then."

("Just an innocent slip, I assure you. I have no intention of taking over. That would be quite immoral.")

Dalt laughed grimly. "What would an ex-slug know about morality?"

("With the aid of your faculties I can reason now, can I not? And if I can reason, why can't I arrive at a moral code? This is your body and I am here only because of blind instinct. I have the ability to take control—not without a struggle, of course—but it would be immoral to attempt to do so. I couldn't vacate your mind if I wanted to, so you're stuck with me, Steve. Might as well make the best of it.")

"We'll see how 'stuck' I am when I get back to the ship," Dalt muttered. "But I'd like to know how you got into my brain."

("I'm not exactly sure of that myself. I know the path I followed to penetrate your skull—if you had the anatomical vocabulary I could describe it to you, but my vocabulary is your vocabulary and yours is very limited in that area.")

"What do you expect? I was educated in cultural studies, not medicine!"

("It's not important anyway. I remember almost nothing of my existence before entering your skull, for it wasn't until then that I first became truly aware.")

Dalt glanced at the console and straightened up in his seat. "Well, whatever you are, go away for now. I'm ready to dock and I don't want to be distracted."

("Gladly. You have a most fascinating organism and I have much exploring to do before I become fully acquainted with it. So long for now, Steve. It's nice knowing you.")

A thought drifted through Dalt's head: *If I'm going nuts, at least I'm not doing it halfheartedly!*

II

BARRE WAS THERE to meet him at the dock. "No luck, Steve?"

Dalt shook his head and was about to add a comment when he noticed Barre staring at him with a strange expression.

"What's the matter?"

"You won't believe me if I tell you," Barre replied. He took Dalt's arm and led him into a nearby men's room and stood him in front of a mirror.

Dalt saw what he expected to see: a tall, muscular man in the garb of a Kwashi serf. Tanned face, short, glossy brown hair . . . Dalt suddenly flexed his neck to get a better look at the top of his head. Tufts of hair were missing in a roughly oval patch on his scalp. He ran his hand over it and a light rain of brown hair showered past his eyes. With successive strokes, the oval patch became completely denuded and a shiny expanse of scalp reflected the ceiling lights into the mirror.

"Well, I'll be damned! A bald spot!"

("Don't worry, Steve,") said the voice in his head, ("the roots aren't dead. The hair will grow back.")

"It damn well better!" Dalt said aloud.

"It damn well better what?" Barre asked puzzledly.

"Nothing," Dalt replied. "Something dropped onto

11

my head in a cave down there and it looks like it's given me a bald spot." He realized then that he would have to be very careful about talking to his invader; otherwise, even if he really wasn't crazy, he'd soon have everyone on the ship believing he was.

"Maybe you'd better see the doc," Barre suggested.

"I intend to, believe me. But first I've got to report to Clarkson. I'm sure he's waiting."

"You can bet on it." Barre had been a research head on the brain project and was well acquainted with Dirval Clarkson's notorious impatience.

The pair walked briskly toward Clarkson's office. The rotation of the huge conical ship gave the effect of one-G.

"Hi, Jean," Dalt said with a smile as he and Barre entered the anteroom of Clarkson's office. Jean was Clarkson's secretary-receptionist and she and Dalt had entertained each other on the trip out . . . the more interesting games had been played during the sleeptime hours.

She returned his smile. "Glad you're back in one piece." Dalt realized that from her seated position she couldn't see the bald spot. Just as well for the moment. He'd explain it to her later.

Jean spoke into the intercom: "Mr. Dalt is here."

"Well, send him in!" squawked a voice. "Send him in!"

Dalt grinned and pushed through the door to Clarkson's office, with Barre trailing behind. A huge, graying man leaped from behind a desk and stalked forward at a precarious angle.

"Dalt! Where the hell have you been? You were supposed to go down, take a look, and then come back up. You could have done the procedure three times in the period you took. And what happened to your head?" Clarkson's speech was in its usual rapidfire form.

"Well, this—"

"Never mind that now! What's the story? I can tell right now that you didn't find anything, because Barre is with you. If you'd found the brain he'd be off in some corner now nursing it like a misplaced infant! Well, tell me! How does it look?"

Dalt hesitated, not quite sure whether the barrage had come to an end. "It doesn't look good," he said finally.

"And why not?"

"Because I couldn't find a trace of the ship itself. Oh, there's evidence of some sort of craft having been there a while back, but it must have gotten off-planet again, because there's not a trace of wreckage to be found."

Clarkson looked puzzled. "Not even a trace?"

"Nothing."

The project director pondered this a moment, then shrugged. "We'll have to figure that one out later. But right now you should know that we picked up another signal from the brain's life-support system while you were off on your joyride—"

"It wasn't a joyride," Dalt declared. A few moments with Clarkson always managed to rub his nerves raw. "I ran into a pack of unfriendly locals and had to hide in a cave."

"Be that as it may," Clarkson said, returning to his desk chair, "we're now certain that the brain, or what's left of it, is on Kwashi."

"Yes, but where on Kwashi? It's not exactly an asteroid, you know."

"We've almost pinpointed its location," Barre broke in excitedly. "Very close to the site you inspected."

"It's in Bendelema, I hope," Dalt said.

"Why?" Clarkson asked.

"Because when I was on cultural survey down there I posed as a soldier of fortune—a mercenary of sorts—and Duke Kile of Bendelema was a former employer. I'm known and liked in Bendelema. I'm not at all popular in Tependia because they're the ones I fought against. I repeat: It's in Bendelema, I hope."

Clarkson nodded. "It's in Bendelema."

"Good!" Dalt exhaled with relief. "That makes everything much simpler. I've got an identity in Bendelema: Racso the mercenary. At least that's a starting place."

"And you'll start tomorrow," Clarkson said. "We've wasted too much time as it is. If we don't get that prototype back and start coming up with some pretty good reasons for the malfunction, Star Ways just might cancel the project. There's a lot riding on you, Dalt. Remember that."

Dalt turned toward the door. "Who'll let me forget?" he remarked with a grim smile. "I'll check in with you before I leave."

"Good enough," Clarkson said with a curt nod, then turned to Barre. "Hold on a minute, Barre. I want to go over a few things with you." Dalt gladly closed the door on the pair.

"It's almost lunchtime," said a feminine voice behind him. "How about it?"

In a single motion, Dalt spun, leaned over Jean's desk, and gave her a peck on the lips. "Sorry, can't. It may be noon to all of you on ship-time, but it's some hellish hour of the morning to me. I've got to drop in on the doc, then I've just got to get some sleep."

But Jean wasn't listening. Instead, she was staring fixedly at the bald spot on Dalt's head. "Steve!" she cried. "What happened?"

Dalt straightened up abruptly. "Nothing much. Something landed on it while I was below and the hair fell out. It'll grow back, don't worry."

"I'm not worried about that," she said, standing up and trying to get another look. But Dalt kept his head high. "Did it hurt?"

"Not at all. Look, I hate to run off like this, but I've got to get some sleep. I'm going back down tomorrow."

Her face fell. "So soon?"

"I'm afraid so. Why don't we make it for dinner tonight. I'll drop by your room and we'll go from there. The caf isn't exactly a restaurant, but if we get there late we can probably have a table all to ourselves."

"And after that?" she asked coyly.

"I'll be damned if we're going to spend my last night on ship for who-knows-how-long in the vid theater!"

Jean smiled. "I was hoping you'd say that."

("What odd physiological rumblings that female stirs in you!") the voice said as Dalt walked down the corridor to the medical offices. He momentarily broke stride at the sound of it. He'd almost forgotten that he had company.

"That's none of your business!" he muttered through tight lips.

("I'm afraid much of what you do is my business. I'm not directly connected with you emotionally, but physically . . . what you feel, I feel; what you see, I see; what you taste—")

"Okay! Okay!"

("You're holding up rather well, actually. Better than I would have expected.")

"Probably my cultural-survey training. They taught me how to keep my reactions under control when faced with an unusual situation."

("Glad to hear it. We may well have a long relationship ahead of us if you don't go the way of most high-order intelligences and suicidally reject me. We can look on your body as a small business and the two of us as partners.")

"Partners!" Dalt said, somewhat louder than he wished. Luckily, the halls were deserted. "This is *my* body!"

("If it will make you happier, I'll revise my analogy: You're the founder of the company and I've just bought my way in. How's that sound, Partner?")

"Lousy!"

("Get used to it,") the voice singsonged.

"Why bother? You won't be in there much longer. The doc'll see to that!"

("He won't find a thing, Steve.")

"We'll see."

The door to the medical complex swished open when Dalt touched the operating plate and he passed into a tiny waiting room.

"What can we do for you, Mr. Dalt?" the nurse-receptionist said. Dalt was a well-known figure about the ship by now.

He inclined his head toward the woman and pointed to the bald spot. "I want to see the doc about this. I'm going below tomorrow and I want to get this cleared up before I do. So if the doc's got a moment, I'd like to see him."

The nurse smiled. "Right away." At the moment, Dalt was a very important man. He was the only one on ship legally allowed on Kwashi. If he thought he needed a doctor, he'd have one.

A man in a traditional white medical coat poked his head through one of the three doors leading from the waiting room, in answer to the nurse's buzz.

"What is it, Lorraine?" he asked.

"Mr. Dalt would like to see you, Doctor."

He glanced at Dalt. "Of course. Come in, Mr. Dalt. I'm Dr. Graves." The doctor showed him into a small, book-and-microfilm-lined office. "Have a seat, will you? I'll be with you in a minute."

Graves exited by another door and Dalt was alone . . . almost.

("He has quite an extensive library here, doesn't he?") said the voice. Dalt glanced at the shelves and noticed printed texts that must have been holdovers from the doctor's student days and microfilm spools of the latest clinical developments. ("You would do me a great service by asking the doctor if you could borrow some of his more basic texts.")

"What for? I thought you knew all about me."

("I know quite a bit now, it's true, but I'm still learning and I'll need a vocabulary to explain things to you now and then.")

"Forget it. You're not going to be around that long."

Dr. Graves entered then. "Now. What seems to be the problem, Mr. Dalt?"

Dalt explained the incident in the cave. "Legend has it—and colonial experience seems to confirm it—that 'of every thousand struck down, nine hundred and

ninety-nine will die.' I was floored by an alaret but I'm
still kicking and I'd like to know why.''

(''I believe I've already explained that by luck of a
random constitutional factor, your nervous system
didn't reject me.'')

Shut up! Dalt mentally snarled.

The doctor shrugged. ''I don't see the problem.
You're alive and all you've got to show for your en-
counter is a bald spot, and even that will disappear—it's
bristly already. I can't tell you why you're alive because
I don't know how these alarets kill their victims. As far
as I know, no one's done any research on them. So why
don't you just forget about it and stay out of caves.''

''It's not that simple, Doc.'' Dalt spoke carefully.
He'd have to phrase things just right; if he came right
out and told the truth, he'd sound like a flaming schiz.
''I have this feeling that something seeped into my
scalp, maybe even into my head. I feel this thickness
there.'' Dalt noticed the slightest narrowing of the doctor's gaze. ''I'm not crazy,'' he said hurriedly. ''You've
got to admit that the alaret did something up there—the
bald spot proves it. Couldn't you make a few tests or
something? Just to ease my mind.''

The doctor nodded. He was satisfied that Dalt's fears
had sufficient basis in reality, and the section-eight
gleam left his eyes. He led Dalt into the adjoining room
and placed a cubical helmetlike apparatus over his head.
A click, a buzz, and the helmet was removed. Dr.
Graves pulled out two small transparencies and shoved
them into a viewer. The screen came to life with two
views of the inside of Dalt's skull: a lateral and an
anterior-posterior.

''Nothing to worry about,'' he said after a moment of
study. ''I scanned you for your own piece of mind. Take
a look.''

Dalt looked, even though he didn't know what he was
looking for.

(''I told you so,'') said the voice. (''I'm thoroughly
integrated with your nervous system.'')

''Well, thanks for your trouble, Doc. I guess I've

really got nothing to worry about," Dalt lied.

"Nothing at all. Just consider yourself lucky to be alive if those alarets are as deadly as you say."

("Ask him for the books!") the voice said.

I'm going to sleep as soon as I leave here. You won't get a chance to read them.

("You let me worry about that. Just get the books for me.")

Why should I do you any favors?

("Because I'll see to it that you have one difficult time of getting to sleep. I'll keep repeating 'get the books, get the books, get the books' until you finally do it.")

I believe you would!

("You can count on it.")

"Doc," Dalt said, "would you mind lending me a few of your books?"

"Like what?"

"Oh, anatomy and physiology, to start."

Dr. Graves walked into the other room and took two large, frayed volumes from the shelves. "What do you want 'em for?"

"Nothing much," Dalt said, taking the books and tucking them under his arm. "Just want to look up a few things."

"Well, just don't forget where you got them. And don't let that incident with the alaret become an obsession with you," the doc said meaningfully.

Dalt smiled. "I've already banished it from my mind."

("That's a laugh!")

Dalt wasted no time in reaching his quarters after leaving the medical offices. He was on the bed before the door could slide back into the closed position. Putting the medical books on the night table, he buried his face in the pillow and immediately dropped off to sleep.

He awoke five hours later, feeling completely refreshed except for his eyes. They felt hot, burning.

("You may return those books anytime you wish,") the voice said.

"Lost interest already?" Dalt yawned, stretching as he lay on the bed.

("In a way, yes. I read them while you were asleep.")

"How the hell did you do that?"

("Quite simple, really. While your mind was sleeping, I used your eyes and your hands to read. I digested the information and stored it away in your brain. By the way, there's an awful lot of wasted space in the human brain. You're not living up to anywhere near your potential, Steve. Neither is any other member of your race, I gather.")

"What right have you got to pull something like that with my body?" Dalt said angrily. He sat up and rubbed his eyes.

("*Our* body, you mean.")

Dalt ignored that. "No wonder my eyes are burning! I've been reading when I could have been—*should* have been—sleeping!"

("Don't get excited. You got your sleep and I built up my vocabulary. You're fully rested, so what's your complaint? By the way, I can now tell you how I entered your head. I seeped into your pores and then into your scalp capillaries, which I followed into your parietal emissary veins. These flow through the parietal for-amina in your skull and empty into the superior sagittal sinus. From there it was easy to infiltrate your central nervous system.")

Dalt opened his mouth to say that he really didn't care, when he realized that he understood exactly what the voice was saying. He had a clear picture of the de-scribed path floating through his mind.

"How come I know what you're talking about? I seem to understand but I don't remember ever hearing those terms before . . . and then again, I do. It's weird."

("It must seem rather odd,") the voice concurred. ("What has happened is that I've made my new knowledge available to you. The result is you experience the fruits of the learning process without having gone through it. You know facts without remembering hav-ing learned them.")

"Well," Dalt said, rising to his feet, "at least you're not a complete parasite."

("I resent that! We're partners . . . a symbiosis!")

"I suppose you may come in handy now and then." Dalt sighed.

("I already have.")

"What's that supposed to mean?"

("I found a small neoplasm in your lung—middle lobe on the right. It might well have become malignant.")

"Then let's get back to the doc before it metastatizes!" Dalt said, and idly realized that a few hours ago he would have been worrying about "spread" rather than "metastasis."

("There's no need to worry, Steve. I killed it off.")

"How'd you do that?"

("I just worked through your vascular system and selectively cut off the blood supply to that particular group of cells.")

"Well, thanks, Partner."

("No thanks necessary, I assure you. I did it for my own good as well as yours—I don't relish the idea of walking around in a cancer-ridden body any more than you do!")

Dalt removed his serf clothing in silence. The enormity of what had happened in that cave on Kwashi struck him now with full force. He had a built-in medical watchdog who would keep everything running smoothly. He smiled grimly as he donned ship clothes and suspended from his neck the glowing prismatic gem that he had first worn as Racso and had continued to wear after his cultural-survey assignment on Kwashi had been terminated. He'd have his health but he'd lost his privacy forever. He wondered if it was worth it.

("One other thing, Steve,") said the voice. ("I've accelerated the growth of your hair in the bald spot to maximum.")

Dalt put up a hand and felt a thick fuzz where before there had been only bare scalp. "Hey! You're right! It's

really coming in!'' He went to the mirror to take a look.
''Oh, no!''

(''Sorry about that, Steve. I couldn't see it so I wasn't
aware there had been a color change. I'm afraid there's
nothing I can do about that.'')

Dalt stared in dismay at the patch of silvery gray in
the center of his otherwise inky hair. ''I look like a
freak!''

(''You can always dye it.'')

Dalt made a disgusted noise.

(''I have a few questions, Steve,'') the voice said in a
hasty attempt to change the subject.

''What about?''

(''About why you're going down to that planet tomorrow.'')

''I'm going because I was once a member of the
Federation cultural-survey team on Kwashi and because
the Star Ways Corporation lost an experimental pilot
brain down there. They got permission from the Federation to retrieve the brain only on the condition that a
cultural-survey man does the actual retrieving.''

(''That's not what I meant. I want to know what's so
important about the brain, just how much of a brain it
actually is, and so on.'')

''There's an easy way to find out,'' Dalt said, heading
for the door. ''We'll just go to the ship's library.''

The library was near the hub of the ship and completely computer-operated. Dalt closed himself away in
one of the tiny viewer booths and pushed his ID card
into the awaiting slot.

The flat, dull tones of the computer's voice came
from a hidden speaker.

''What do you wish, Mr. Dalt?''

''I might as well go the route: Let me see everything
on the brain project.''

Four microspools slid down a tiny chute and landed
in the receptacle in front of Dalt. ''I'm sorry, Mr.
Dalt,'' said the computer, ''but this is all your present
status allows you to see.''

("That should be enough, Steve. Feed them into the viewer.")

The story that unraveled from the spools was one of biologic and economic daring. Star Ways was fast achieving what amounted to a monopoly of the interstellar-warp-unit market and from there was expanding to peristellar drive. But unlike the typical established corporation, SW was pouring money into basic research. One of the prime areas of research was the development of a use for cultured human neural tissue. And James Barre had found a use that held great economic potential.

The prime expense of interstellar commercial travel, whether freight or passenger, was the crew. Good spacers were a select lot and hard to come by; running a ship took a lot of them. There had been many attempts to replace crews with computers but these had invariably failed due either to mass/volume problems or overwhelming maintenance costs. Barre's development of an "artificial" brain—by that he meant structured in vitro—seemed to hold an answer, at least for cargo ships.

After much trial and error with life-support systems and control linkages, a working prototype had finally been developed. A few short hops had been tried with a full crew standing by, and the results had been more than anyone had hoped for. So the prototype was prepared for a long interstellar journey with five scheduled stops—with cargo holds empty, of course. The run had gone quite well until the ship got into the Kwashi area. A single technician had been sent along to insure that nothing went too far awry, and, according to his story, he was sitting in his quarters when the ship suddenly came out of warp with the emergency/abandon ship signals blaring. He wasted no time in getting to a lifeboat and ejecting. The ship made a beeline for Kwashi and disappeared, presumably in a crash. That had been eight months ago.

No more information was available without special clearance.

"Well, that was a waste of time," Dalt said.

"Are you addressing me, Mr. Dalt?" the computer asked.

"No."

("There certainly wasn't much new information there,") the voice agreed.

Dalt pulled his card from the slot, thereby cutting the computer off from this particular viewer booth, before answering. Otherwise it would keep butting in.

"The theories now stand at either malfunction or foul play."

("Why foul play?")

"The spacers' guild, for one," Dalt said, standing. "Competing companies, for another. But since it crashed on a restricted splinter world, I favor the malfunction theory." As he stepped from the booth he glanced at the chronometer on the wall: 1900 hours shiptime. Jean would be waiting.

The cafeteria was nearly deserted when he arrived with Jean and the pair found an isolated table in a far corner.

"I really don't think you should dye your hair at all," Jean was saying as they placed their trays on the table and sat down. "I think that gray patch looks cute in a distinguished sort of way . . . or do I mean distinguished in a cute sort of way?"

Dalt took the ribbing in good-natured silence.

"Steve!" she said suddenly. "How come you're eating with your left hand? I've never seen you do that before."

Dalt looked down. His fork was firmly grasped in his left hand. "That's strange," he said. "I didn't even realize it."

("I integrated a few circuits, so to speak, while you were asleep,") the voice said. ("It seemed rather ridiculous to favor one limb over another. You're now ambidextrous.")

Thanks for telling me, Partner!

("Sorry. I forgot.")

Dalt switched the fork to his right hand and Jean
switched the topic of conversation.

"You know, Steve," she said, "you've never told me
why you quit the cultural-survey group."

Dalt paused before answering. After the fall of Metep
VII, last in a long line of self-styled "Emperors of the
Outworlds," a new independent spirit gave rise to a
loose organization of worlds called simply the Federation.

"As you know," he said finally, "the Federation has
a long-range plan of bringing splinter worlds—willing
ones, that is—back into the fold. But it was found that
an appalling number had regressed into barbarism. So
the cultural surveys were started to evaluate splinter
worlds and decide which could be trusted with modern
technology. There was another rule which I didn't fully
appreciate back then but have come to believe in since,
and that's where the trouble began."

"What rule was that?"

"It's not put down anywhere in so many words, but it
runs to the effect that if any splinter-world culture has
started developing on a path at variance with the rest of
humanity, it is to be left alone."

"Sounds like they were making cultural test tubes out
of some planets," Jean said.

"Exactly what I thought, but it never bothered me
until I surveyed a planet that must, for now, remain
nameless. The inhabitants had been developing a psi
culture through selective breeding and were actually developing a tangential society. In my report I strongly
recommended admission to the Fed; I thought we could
learn as much from them as they from us."

"But it was turned down, I bet," Jean concluded.

Dalt nodded. "I had quite a row with my superiors
but they held firm and I stalked out in a rage and quit."

"Maybe they thought you were too easy on the
planet."

"They knew better. I had no qualms about proscrib-
ing Kwashi, for instance. No, their reason was fear that
the psi society was not mature enough to be exposed to

galactic civilization, that it would be swallowed up. They wanted to give it another century or two. I thought that was unfair but was powerless to do anything about it."

Jean eyed him with a penetrating gaze. "I notice you've been using the past tense. Change your mind since then?"

"Definitely. I've come to see that there's a very basic, very definite philosophy behind everything the Federation does. It not only wants to preserve human diversity, it wants to see it stretched to the limit. Man was an almost completely homogenized species before he began colonizing the stars; interstellar travel arrived just in time. Old Earth is still a good example of what I mean; long ago the Eastern and Western Alliances fused—something no one ever thought would happen—and Earth is just one big faceless, self-perpetuating bureaucracy. The populace is equally faceless.

"But the man who left for the stars—he's another creature altogether! Once he got away from the press of other people, once he stopped seeing what everybody else saw, hearing what everybody else heard, he began to become an individual again and to strike out in directions of his own choosing. The splinter groups carried this out to an extreme and many failed. But a few survived and the Federation wants to let the successful ones go as far as they can, both for their own sake and for the sake of all mankind. Who knows? *Homo superior* may one day be born on a splinter world."

They took their time strolling back to Dalt's quarters. Once inside, Dalt glanced in the mirror and ran his hand through the gray patch in his hair. "It's still there," he muttered in mock disappointment.

He turned back to Jean and she was already more than half undressed. "You weren't gone all that long, Steve," she said in a low voice, "but I missed you—really missed you."

It was mutual.

III

SHE WAS GONE when he awakened the next morning but a little note on the night table wished him good luck.

("You should have prepared me for such a sensory jolt,") said the voice. ("I was taken quite by surprise last night.")

"Oh, it's you again." Dalt groaned. "I pushed you completely out of my mind last night, otherwise I'd have been impotent, no doubt."

("I hooked into your sensory input—very stimulating.")

Dalt experienced helpless annoyance. He would have to get used to his partner's presence at the most intimate moments, but how many people could make love knowing that there's a peeping tom at the window with a completely unobstructed view?

("What are we going to do now?")

"Pard," Dalt drawled, "we're gonna git ready to go below." He went to the closet and pulled from it a worn leather jerkin and a breastplate marked with an empty red circle, the mark of the mercenary. Stiff leather breeches followed and broadsword and metal helm completed the picture. He then dyed his hair for Racso's sake.

"One more thing," he said, and reached up to the far end of the closet shelf. His hand returned clutching an

ornate dagger. "This is something new in Racso's arma-
ment."

("A dagger?")

"Not just a dagger. It's—"

("Oh, yes. It's also a blaster.")

"How did you know?"

("We're partners, Steve. What you know, I know. I
even know why you had it made.")

"I'm listening."

("Because you're afraid you're not as fast as you used
to be. You think your muscles may not have quite the
tone they used to have when you first posed as Racso.
And you're not willing to die looking for an artificial
brain.")

"You seem to think you know me pretty well."

("I do. Skin to skin, birth to now. You're the only
son of a fairly well-to-do couple on Friendly, had an
average childhood and an undistinguished academic
career—but you passed the empathy test with high
marks and were accepted into the Federation cultural-
survey service. You don't speak to your parents anymore. They've never forgiven their baby for running off
to go hopping from splinter world to splinter world.
You cut yourself off from your home-world but made
friends in CS; now you're cut off from CS. You're not a
loner by nature but you've adapted. In fact, you have a
tremendous capacity to adapt as long as your own personal code of ethics and honor isn't violated—you're
very strict about that.")

Dalt sighed. "No secrets anymore, I guess."

("Not from me, at least.")

Dalt planned the time of his arrival in Bendelema
Duchy for predawn. He concealed the shuttler and was
on the road as the sky began to lighten. Walking with a
light saddle slung over his shoulder, he marveled at the
full ripe fields of grains and greens on either side of him.
Agriculture had always been a hit-or-miss affair on
Kwashi and famines were not uncommon, but it looked
as if there would be no famine in Bendelema this year.

Even the serfs looked well fed.

"What do you think, Pard?" Dalt asked.

("Well, Kwashi hasn't got much of a tilt on its axis. They seem to be on their way to the second bumper crop of the year.")

"With the available farming methods, that's unheard of . . . I almost starved here once myself."

("I know that, but I have no explanation for these plump serfs.")

The road made a turn around a small wooded area and the Bendelema keep came into view.

"I see their architecture hasn't improved since I left. The keep still looks like a pile of rocks."

("I wonder why so many retrograde splinter worlds turn to feudalism?") Pard said as they approached the stone structure.

"There are only theories. Could be that feudalism is, in essence, the law of the jungle. When these colonists first land, education of the children has to take a back seat to putting food on the table. That's their first mistake and a tragic one, because once they let technology slide, they're on a downhill spiral. Usually by the third generation you have a pretty low technological level; the stops are out, the equalizers are gone, and the toughs take over.

"The philosophy of feudalism is one of muscle: Mine is what I can take and hold. It's ordered barbarism. That's why feudal worlds such as Kwashi have to be kept out of the Federation—can you imagine a bunch of these yahoos in command of an interstellar dreadnaught? No one's got the time or the money to reeducate them, so they just have to be left alone to work out their own little industrial revolution and so forth. When they're ready, the Fed will give them the option of joining up."

"Ho, mercenary!" someone hailed from the keep gate. "What do you seek in Bendelema?"

"Have I changed that much, Farri?" Dalt answered.

The guard peered at him intensely from the wall, then his face brightened. "Racso! Enter and be welcome!

The Duke has need of men of your mettle."

Farri, a swarthy trooper who had gained a few pounds and a few scars since their last meeting, greeted him as he passed through the open gate. "Where's your mount, Racso?" He grinned. "You were never one to walk when you could ride."

"Broke its leg in a ditch more miles back then I care to remember. Had to kill it . . . good steed, too."

"That's a shame. But the Duke'll see that you get a new one."

Dalt's audience with the Duke was disturbingly brief. The lord of the keep had not been as enthusiastic as expected. Dalt couldn't decide whether to put the man's reticence down to distraction with other matters or to suspicion. His son Anthon was a different matter, however. He was truly glad to see Racso.

"Come," he said after mutual greetings were over. "We'll put you in the room next to mine upstairs."

"For a mercenary?"

"For my teacher!" Anthon had filled out since Dalt had seen him last. He had spent many hours with the lad, passing on the tricks of the blade he had learned in his own training days. "I've used your training well, Racso!"

"I hope you didn't stop learning when I left," Dalt said.

"Come down to the sparring field and you'll see that I've not been lax in your absence. I'm a match for you now."

He was more than a match. What he lacked in skill and subtlety he made up with sheer ferocity. Dalt was several times hard-pressed to defend himself, but in the general stroke-and-parry, give-and-take exercises of the practice session he studied Anthon. The lad was still the same as he had remembered him, on the surface: bold, confident, the Duke's only legitimate son and heir to Bendelema, yet there was a new undercurrent. Anthon had always been brutish and a trifle cruel, perfect qualities for a future feudal lord, but there was now an added note of desperation. Dalt hadn't noticed it before and could think of no reason for its presence now. Anthon's position was secure—what was driving him?

After the workout, Dalt immersed himself in a huge tub of hot water, a habit that had earned him the reputation of being a little bit odd the last time around, and then retired to his quarters, where he promptly fell asleep. The morning's long walk carrying the saddle, followed by the vigorous swordplay with Anthon, had drained him.

He awoke feeling stiff and sore.

("I hope those aching muscles cause you sufficient misery.")

"Why do you say that, Pard?" Dalt asked as he kneaded the muscles in his sword arm.

("Because you weren't ready for a workout like that. The clumsy practicing you did on the ship didn't prepare you for someone like Anthon. It's all right if you want to make yourself sore, but don't forget I feel it, too!")

"Well, just cut off pain sensations. You can do it, can't you?"

("Yes, but that's almost as unpleasant as the aching itself.")

"You'll just have to suffer along with me then. And by the way, you've been awful quiet today. What's up?"

("I've been observing, comparing your past impressions of Bendelema keep with what we see now. Either you're a rotten observer or something's going on here . . . something suspicious or something secret or I don't know what.")

"What do you mean by 'rotten observer'?"

("I mean that either your past observations were inaccurate or Bendelema has changed.")

"In what way?"

("I'm not quite sure as yet, but I should know before long. I'm a far more astute observer than you—")

Dalt threw his hands up with a groan. "Not only do I have a live-in busy-body, but an arrogant one to boot!"

There was a knock on the door.

"Come in," Dalt said.

The door opened and Anthon entered. He glanced about the room. "You're alone? I thought I heard you talking—"

"A bad habit of mine of late," Dalt explained hastily. "I think out loud."

Anthon shrugged. "The evening meal will soon be served and I've ordered a place set for you at my father's table. Come."

As he followed the younger man down a narrow flight of roughhewn steps, Dalt caught the heavy, unmistakable scent of Kwashi wine.

A tall, cadaverous man inclined his head as they passed into the dining hall. "Hello, Strench," Dalt said with a smile. "Still the majordomo, I see."

"As long as His Lordship allows," Strench replied.

The Duke himself entered not far behind them and all present remained standing until His Lordship was seated. Dalt found himself near the head of the table and guessed by the ruffled appearance of a few of the court advisers that they had been pushed a little farther from the seat of power than they liked.

"I must thank His Lordship for the honor of allowing a mercenary to sup at his table," Dalt said after a court official had made the customary toast to Bendelema and the Duke's longevity.

"Nonsense, Racso," the Duke replied. "You served me well against Tependia and you've always taken a wholesome interest in my son. You know you will always find welcome in Bendelema."

Dalt inclined his head.

("Why are you bowing and scraping to this slob?")

Shut up, Pard! It's all part of the act.

("But don't you realize how many serfs this barbarian oppresses?")

Shut up, self-righteous parasite!

("Symbiote!")

Dalt rose to his feet and lifted his wine cup. "On the subject of your son, I would like to make a toast to the future Duke of Bendelema: Anthon."

With a sudden animal-like cry, Anthon shot to his feet and hurled his cup to the stone floor. Without a word of explanation, he stormed from the room.

The other diners were as puzzled as Dalt. "Perhaps I said the wrong thing. . . ."

"I don't know what it could have been," the Duke said, his eyes on the red splotch of spilled wine that seeped across the stones. "But Anthon has been acting rather strange of late."

Dalt sat down and raised his cup to his lips.

("I wouldn't quaff too deeply of that beverage, my sharp-tongued partner.")

And why not? Dalt thought, casually resting his lips on the brim.

("Because I think there's something in your wine that's not in any of the others' and I think we should be careful.")

What makes you suspicious?

("I told you your powers of observation needed sharpening.")

Never mind that! Explain!

("All right. I noticed that your cup was already filled when it was put before you; everyone else's was poured from that brass pitcher.")

That doesn't sound good, Dalt agreed. He started to put the cup down.

("Don't do that! Just wet your lips with a tiny amount and I think I might be able to analyze it by its effect. A small amount shouldn't cause any real harm.")

Dalt did so and waited.

("Well, at least they don't mean you any serious harm,") Pard said finally. ("Not yet.")

What is it?

("An alkaloid, probably from some local root.")

What's it supposed to do to me?

("Put you out of the picture for the rest of the night.")

Dalt pondered this. *I wonder what for?*

("I haven't the faintest. But while they're all still distracted by Anthon's departure, I suggest you pour your wine out on the floor immediately. It will mix with Anthon's and no one will be the wiser. You may then proceed to amaze these yokels with your continuing consciousness.")

I have a better idea, Dalt thought as he poured the wine along the outside of his boot so that it would strike the floor in a smooth silent flow instead of a noisy splash. *I'll wait a few minutes and then pass out. Maybe that way we'll find out what they've got in mind.*

("Sounds risky.")

Nevertheless, that's what we'll do.

Dalt decided to make the most of the time he had left before passing out. "You know," he said, feigning a deep swallow of wine, "I saw a bright light streak across the sky last night. It fell to earth far beyond the horizon. I've heard tales lately of such a light coming to rest in this region, some even say it landed in Bendelema itself. Is this true or merely the mutterings of vassals in their cups?"

The table chatter ceased abruptly. So did all eating and drinking. Every face at the table stared in Dalt's direction.

"Why do you ask this, Racso?" the Duke said. The curtain of suspicion which had seemed to vanish at the beginning of the meal had again been drawn closed between Racso and the Duke.

Dalt decided it was time for his exit. "My only interest, your Lordship, is in the idle tales I've heard. I . . ." He half rose from his seat and put a hand across his eyes. "I . . ." Carefully, he allowed himself to slide to the floor.

"Carry him upstairs," said the Duke.

"Why don't we put an end to his meddling now, Your Lordship," suggested one of the advisers.

"Because he's a friend of Anthon's and he may well mean us no harm. We will know tomorrow."

With little delicacy and even less regard for his physical well-being, Dalt was carried up to his room and unceremoniously dumped on the bed. The heavy sound of the hardwood door slamming shut was followed by the click of a key in the lock.

Dalt sprang up and checked the door. The key had been taken from the inside and left in the lock after being turned.

("So much for that bright idea,") Pard commented caustically.

"None of your remarks, if you please."

("What do we do, now that we're confined to quarters for the rest of the night?")

"What else?" Dalt said. He kicked off his boots, removed breastplate, jerkin, and breeches, and hopped into bed.

The door was unlocked the next morning and Dalt made his way downstairs as unobtrusively as possible. Strench's cell-like quarters were just off the kitchen, if memory served . . . yes, there it was. And Strench was nowhere about.

("What do you think you're doing?")

I'm doing my best to make sure we don't get stuck up there in that room again tonight. His gaze came to rest on the large board where Strench kept all the duplicate keys for the locks of the keep.

("I begin to understand.")

Slow this morning, aren't you?

Dalt took the duplicate key to his room off its hook and replaced it with another, similar key from another part of the board. Strench might realize at some time during the day that a key was missing, but he'd be looking for the wrong one.

Dalt ran into the majordomo moments later.

"His Lordship wishes to see you, Racso," he said stiffly.

"Where is he?"

"On the North Wall."

("This could be a critical moment.")

"Why do you say that, Pard?" Dalt muttered.

("Remember last night, after you pulled your dramatic collapsing act? The Duke said something about finding out about you today.")

"And you think this could be it?"

("Could be. I'm not sure, of course, but I'm glad you have that dagger in your belt.")

The Duke was alone on the wall and greeted Dalt/Racso as warmly as his aloof manner would permit after the latter apologized for "drinking too much" the night before.

"I'm afraid I have a small confession to make," the Duke said.

"Yes, Your Lordship?"

"I suspected you of treachery when you first arrived." He held up a gloved hand as Dalt opened his mouth to reply. "Don't protest your innocence. I've just heard from a spy in the Tependian court and he says you have not set foot in Tependia since your mysterious disappearance years ago."

Dalt hung his head. "I am grieved, M'Lord."

"Can you blame me, Racso? Everyone knows that you hire out to the highest bidder, and Tependia has taken an inordinate interest in what goes on in Bendelema lately, even to the extent of sending raiding parties into our territory to carry off some of my vassals."

"Why would they want to do that?"

The Duke puffed up with pride. "Because Bendelema has become a land of plenty. As you know, the last harvest was plentiful everywhere; and, as usual, the present crop is stunted everywhere . . . except in Bendelema." Dalt didn't know that but he nodded anyway. So only Bendelema was having a second bumper crop—that was interesting.

"I suppose you have learned some new farming methods and Tependia wants to steal them," Dalt suggested.

"That and more." The Duke nodded. "We also have new storage methods and new planting methods. When the next famine comes, we shall overcome Tependia not with swords and firebrands, but with food! The starving Tependians will leave their lord and Bendelema will extend its boundaries!"

Dalt was tempted to say that if the Tependians were snatching up vassals and stealing Bendelema's secrets, there just might not be another famine. But the Duke was dreaming of empire and it is not always wise for a mere mercenary to interrupt a duke's dreams of empire. Dalt remained silent as the Duke stared at the horizon he soon hoped to own.

The rest of the day was spent in idle search of rumors and by the dinner hour Dalt was sure of one thing: The ship had crashed or landed in the clearing he had inspected a few days before. More than that was known, but the Bendeleman locals were keeping it to themselves —*yes, I saw the light come down; no, I saw nothing else.*

Anthon again offered him a seat at the head table and Dalt accepted. When the Duke was toasted, Dalt took only a tiny sip.

What's the verdict, Pard?

("Same as last night.")

I wonder what this is all about. They don't drug me at lunch or breakfast—why only at dinner?

("Tonight we'll try to find out.")

Since there was no outburst from Anthon this time, Dalt was hard put to find a way to get rid of his drugged wine. He finally decided to feign a collapse again and spill his cup in the process, hoping to hide the fact that he had taken only a few drops.

After slumping forward on the table, he listened intently.

"How long is this to go on, Father? How can we drug him every night without arousing his suspicions?" It was Anthon's voice.

"As long as you insist on quartering him here instead of with the other men-at-arms!" the Duke replied angrily. "We cannot have him wandering about during the nightly services. He's an outsider and must not learn of the godling!"

Anthon's voice was sulky. "Very well . . . I'll have him move out to the barracks tomorrow."

"I'm sorry, Anthon," the Duke said in a milder tone.

"I know he's a friend of yours, but the godling must come before a mercenary."

("I have a pretty good idea of the nature of this godling,") Pard said as Dalt/Racso was carried upstairs.

The brain? I was thinking that, too. But how would the brain communicate with these people? The prototype wasn't set up for it.

("Why do you drag in communication? Isn't it enough that it came from heaven?")

No. The brain doesn't look godlike in the least. It would have to communicate with the locals before they'd deify it. Otherwise, the crash of the ship would be just another fireside tale for the children.

In a rerun of the previous night's events, Dalt was dumped on his bed and the door was locked from the outside. He waited a few long minutes until everything was silent beyond the door, then he poked the duplicate key into the lock. The original was pushed out on the other side and landed on the stone floor with a nightmarishly loud *clang*. But no other sounds followed, so Dalt twisted his own key and slinked down the hall to the stairway that overlooked the dining area.

Empty. The plates hadn't even been cleared away.

"Now where'd everybody go?" Dalt muttered.

("Quiet! Hear those voices?")

Dalt moved down the stairs, listening. A muted chanting seemed to fill the chamber. A narrow door stood open to his left and the chanting grew louder as he approached it.

This is it . . . they must have gone through here.

The passage within, hewn from earth and rock, led downward and Dalt followed it. Widely spaced torches sputtered flickering light against the rough walls and the chanting grew louder as he moved.

Can you make out what they're saying?

("Something about the sacred objects, half of which must be placed in communion with the sun one day and the other half placed in communion with the sun the next day . . . a continuous cycle.")

The chant suddenly ended.

("It appears the litany is over. We had better go back.")

No, we're hiding right here. The brain is no doubt in there and I want to get back to civilization as soon as possible.

Dalt crouched in a shadowed sulcus in the wall and watched as the procession passed, the Duke in the lead, carrying some cloth-covered objects held out before him, Anthon sullenly following. The court advisers plucked the torches from the walls as they moved, but Dalt noticed that light still bled from the unexplored end of the passage. He sidled along the wall toward it after the others had passed.

He was totally unprepared for the sight that greeted his eyes as he entered the terminal alcove.

It was surreal. The vaulted subterranean chamber was strewn with the wreckage of the lost cargo ship. Huge pieces of twisted metal lay stacked against the walls; smaller pieces hung suspended from the ceiling. And foremost and center, nearly indistinguishable from the other junk, sat the silvery life-support apparatus of the brain, as high as a man and twice as broad.

And atop that—the brain, a ball of neural tissue floating in a nutrient bath within a crystalline globe.

("You can't hear him, can you?") Pard said.

"Him? Him who?"

("The brain—it pictures itself as a him—did manage to communicate with the locals. You were right about that.")

"What are you talking about?"

("It's telepathic, Steve, and my presence in your brain seems to have blocked your reception. I sensed a few impulses back in the passage but I wasn't sure until it greeted us.")

"What's it saying?"

("The obvious: It wants to know who we are and what we want.") There was a short pause. ("Oh, oh! I just told it that we're here to take it back to SW and it let out a telepathic emergency call—a loud one. Don't be surprised if we have company in a few minutes.")

"Great! Now what do we do?" Dalt fingered the dagger in his belt as he pondered the situation. It was already too late to run and he didn't want to have to blast his way out. His eyes rested on the globe.

"Correct me if I'm wrong, Pard, but I seem to remember something about the globe being removable."

("Yes, it can be separated from the life-support system for about two hours with no serious harm to the brain.")

"That's just about all we'd need to get it back to the mothership and hooked up to another unit."

("He's quite afraid, Steve,") Pard said as Dalt began to disconnect the globe. ("By the way, I've figured out that little litany we just heard: The sacred objects that are daily put in 'communion with the sun' are solar batteries. Half are charged one day, half the next. That's how he keeps himself going.")

Dalt had just finished stoppering the globe's exchange ports when the Duke and his retinue arrived in a noisy, disorganized clatter.

"Racso!" the Duke cried on sight of him. "So you've betrayed us after all!"

"I'm sorry," Dalt said, "but this belongs to someone else."

Anthon lunged to the front. "Treacherous scum! And I called you friend!" As the youth's hand reached for his sword hilt, Dalt raised the globe.

"Stay your hand, Anthon! If any of you try to bar my way, I'll smash this globe and your godling with it!" The Duke blanched and laid a restraining hand on his son's shoulder. "I didn't come here with the idea of stealing something from you, but steal it I must. I regret the necessity." Dalt wasn't lying. He felt, justifiably, that he had betrayed a trust and it didn't sit well with him, but he kept reminding himself that the brain belonged to SW and he was only returning it to them.

("I hope your threat holds them,") Pard said. ("If

they consider the possibilities, they'll realize that if they jump you, they'll lose their godling; but if they let you go, they lose it anyway.")

At that moment Anthon voiced this same conclusion, but still his father restrained him. "Let him take the godling, my son. It has aided us with its wisdom, the least we can do is guarantee it safe passage."

Dalt grabbed one of the retainers. "You run ahead and ready me a horse—a good one!" He watched him go, then slowly followed the passage back to the dining area. The Duke and his group remained behind in the alcove.

"I wonder what kind of plot they're hatching against me now," Dalt whispered. "Imagine! All the time I spent here never guessing they were telepaths!"

("They're not, Steve.")

"Then how do you communicate with this thing?" he said, glancing at the globe under his arm.

("The brain is an exceptionally strong sender and receiver, that's the secret. These folk are no more telepathic than anyone else.")

Dalt was relieved to find the horse waiting and the gate open. The larger of Kwashi's two moons was well above the horizon and Dalt took the most direct route to his hidden shuttlecraft.

("Just a minute, Steve,") Pard said as Dalt dismounted near the ship's hiding place. ("We seem to have a moral dilemma on our hands.")

"What's that?" Pard had been silent during the entire trip.

("I've been talking to the brain and I think it's become a little more than just a piloting device.")

"Possibly. It crashed, discovered it was telepathic, and tried to make the best of the situation. We're returning it. What's the dilemma?"

("It didn't crash. It sounded the alarm to get rid of the technician and brought the ship down on purpose. And it doesn't want to go back.")

"Well, it hasn't got much choice in the matter. It was made by SW and that's where it's going."

("Steve, it's *pleading* with us!")

"Pleading?"

("Yes. Look, you're still thinking of this thing as a bunch of neurons put together to pilot a ship, but it's developed into something more than that. It's now a *being*, and a thinking, reasoning, volitional one at that! It's no longer a biomechanism, it's an intelligent creature!")

"So you're a philosopher now, is that it?"

("Tell me, Steve. What's Barre going to do when he gets his hands on it?")

Dalt didn't want to answer that one.

("He's no doubt going to dissect it, isn't he?")

"He might not . . . not after he learns it's intelligent."

("Then let's suppose Barre doesn't dissect him—I mean *it* . . . no, I mean *him*. Never mind. If Barre allows it to live, the rest of its life will be spent as an experimental subject. Is that right? Are we justified in delivering it up for that?")

Dalt didn't answer.

("It's not causing any harm. As a matter of fact, it may well help put Kwashi on a quicker road back to civilization. It wants no power. It memorized the ship's library before it crashed and it was extremely happy down there in that alcove, doling out information about fertilizers and crop rotation and so forth and having its batteries charged every day.")

"I'm touched," Dalt muttered sarcastically.

("Joke if you will, but I don't take this lightly.")

"Do you have to be so self-righteous?"

("I'll say no more. You can leave the globe here and the brain will be able to telepathically contact the keep and they'll come out and get it.")

"And what do I tell Clarkson?"

("Simply tell him the truth, up to the final act, and then say that the globe was smashed at the keep when they tried to jump you and you barely escaped with your life.")

"That may kill the brain project, you know. Retrieval of the brain is vital to its continuance."

("That may be so, but it's a risk we'll have to take. If, however, your report states that the brain we were after had developed a consciousness and self-preservation tendencies, a lot of academic interest will surely be generated and research will go on, one way or the other.")

Much to his dismay, Dalt found himself agreeing with Pard, teetering on the brink of gently placing the globe in the grass and walking away, saying to hell with SW.

("It's still pleading with us, Steve. Like a child.")

"All right, dammit!"

Cursing himself for a sucker and a softy, Dalt walked a safe distance from the shuttlecraft and put down the globe.

"But there's a few things we've got to do before we leave here."

("Like what?")

"Like filling in our little friend here on some of the basics of feudal culture, something that I'm sure was not contained in his ship's library."

("He'll learn from experience.")

"That's what I'm afraid of. Without a clear understanding of Kwashi's feudalism, his aid to Bendelema might well unbalance the whole social structure. An overly prosperous duchy is either overcome by jealous, greedy neighbors, or it uses its prosperity to build an army and pursue a plan of conquest. Either course could prove fatal to the brain and further hinder Kwashi's chances for social and technological rehabilitation."

("So what's your plan?")

"A simple one: You'll take all I know about Kwashi and feudalism and feed it to the brain. And you can stress the necessity of finding a means for wider dissemination of its knowledge, such as telepathically dropping bits of information into the heads by passing merchants, minstrels, and vagabonds. If this prosperity can be spread out over a wide area, there'll be less chance of social upheaval. All of Kwashi will benefit in the long run."

Pard complied and began the feeding process. The

brain had a voracious appetite for information and the
process was soon completed. As Dalt rose to his feet, he
heard a rustling in the bushes. Looking up, he saw Anthon striding toward him with a bared sword.

"I've decided to return the godling," Dalt stammered
lamely.

Anthon stopped. "I don't want the filthy thing! As a
matter of fact, I intend to smash it as soon as I finish
with you!" There was a look of incredible hatred in his
eyes, the look of a young man who has discovered that
his friend and admired instructor is a treacherous thief.

"But the godling has seen to it that no one in Bendelema will ever again go hungry!" Dalt said. "Why
destroy it?"

"Because it has also seen to it that no one in the court
of Bendelema will ever look up to me as Duke!"

"They look up to your father. Why not you in your
turn?"

"They look up to my father out of habit!" he
snarled. "But it is the godling who is the source of
authority in Bendelema! And when my father is gone, I
shall be nothing but a puppet."

Dalt now understood Anthon's moodiness: The brain
threatened his position.

"So you followed me not in spite of my threat to
smash the godling but because of it!"

Anthon nodded and began advancing again. "I also
had a score to settle with you, Racso! I couldn't allow
you to betray my trust and the trust of my father and go
unpunished!" With the last word he aimed a vicious
chop at Dalt, who ducked, spun, and dodged out of the
way. He had not been wearing his sword when he left his
room back at the keep, and consequently did not have it
with him now. But he had the dagger.

Anthon laughed at the sight of the tiny blade. "Think
you can stop me with that?"

If you only knew! Dalt thought. He didn't want to
use the blaster, however. He understood Anthon's feelings. If there were only some way he could stun him and
make his escape.

Anthon attacked ferociously now and Dalt was forced to back-peddle. His foot caught on a stone and as he fell he instinctively threw his free hand out for balance. The ensuing events seemed to occur in slow motion. He felt a jarring, crushing, cutting, agonizing pain in his left wrist and saw Anthon's blade bite through it. The hand flew off as if with a life of its own, and a pulsing stream of red shot into the air. Dalt's right hand, too, seemed to take on a life of its own as it reversed the dagger, pointed the butt of the hilt at Anthon, and pressed the hidden stud. An energy bolt, blinding in the darkness, struck him in the chest and he went down without a sound.

Dalt grabbed his forearm. "My hand!" he screamed in agony and horror.

("Give me control!") Pard said urgently.

"My hand!" was all Dalt could say.

(*"Give me control!"*)

Dalt was jolted by this. He relaxed for a second and suddenly found himself an observer in his own body. His right hand dropped the dagger and cupped itself firmly over the bleeding stump, the thumb and fingers digging into the flesh of his forearm, searching for pressure points on the arteries.

His legs straightened as he rose to his feet and calmly walked toward the concealed shuttlecraft. His elbows parted the bushes and jabbed the plate that operated the door to the outer lock.

("I'm glad you didn't lock this up yesterday,") Pard said as the port swung open. There was a first-aid emergency kit inside for situations such as this. The pinky of his right hand was spared from its pressure duty to flip open the lid of the kit and then a container of stat-gel. The right hand suddenly released its grasp and, amid a splatter of blood, the stump of his left arm was forcefully shoved into the gel and held there.

("That should stop the bleeding.") The gel had an immediate clotting effect on any blood that came into contact with it. The thrombus formed would be firm and tough.

Rising, Dalt discovered that his body was his own again. He stumbled outside, weak and disoriented.

"You saved my life, Pard," he mumbled finally. "When I looked at that stump with the blood shooting out, I couldn't move."

("I saved *our* life, Steve.")

He walked over to where Anthon lay with a smoking hole where his chest had been. "I wished to avoid that. It wasn't really fair, you know. He only had a sword. . . ." Dalt was not quite himself yet. The events of the last minute had not yet been absorbed.

("Fair, hell! What does 'fair' mean when someone's trying to kill you?")

But Dalt didn't seem to hear. He began searching the ground. "My hand! Where's my hand? If we bring it back maybe they can replace it!"

("Not a chance, Steve. Necrosis will be in full swing by the time we get to the mothership.")

Dalt sat down. The situation was finally sinking in. "Oh, well," he said resignedly. "They're doing wonderful things with prosthetics these days."

("Prosthetics! We'll grow a *new* one!")

Dalt paused before answering. "A new hand?"

("Of course! You've still got deposits of omnipotential mesenchymal cells here and there in your body. I'll just have them transported to the stump, and with me guiding the process there'll be no problem to rebuilding the hand. It's really too bad you humans have no conscious control over the physiology of your bodies. With the proper direction, the human body is capable of almost anything.")

"You mean I'll have my hand back? Good as new?"

("Good as new. But at the moment I suggest we get into the ship and depart. The brain has called the Duke and it might be a good thing if we weren't here when he arrived.")

"You know," Dalt said as he entered the shuttlecraft and let the port swing to a close behind him, "with you watching over my body, I could live to a ripe old age."

("All I have to do is keep up with the degenerative

changes and you'll live forever.")

Dalt stopped in midstride. "Forever?"

("Of course. The old natives of this planet knew it when they made up that warning for their children: 'Of every thousand struck down, nine hundred and ninety-nine will die.' The obvious conclusion is that the thousandth victim will *not* die.")

"Ever?"

("Well, there's not much I can do if you catch an energy bolt in the chest like Anthon back there. But otherwise, you won't die of old age—I'll see to that. You won't even get old, for that matter.")

The immensity of what Pard was saying suddenly struck Dalt with full force. "In other words," he breathed, "I'm immortal."

("I'd prefer a different pronoun: *We* are immortal.")

"I don't believe it."

("I don't care what you believe. I'm going to keep you alive for a long, long time, Steve, because while *you* live, *I* live, and I've grown very fond of living.")

Dalt did not move, did not reply.

("Well, what are you waiting for? There's a whole galaxy of worlds out there just waiting to be seen and experienced and I'm getting damn sick of this one!")

Dalt smiled. "What's the hurry?"

There was a pause, then: ("You've got a point there, Steve. There's really no hurry at all. We've got all the time in the world. Literally.")

PART TWO:

Heal thy Neighbor

YEAR 218

It is difficult in these times to appreciate the devastating effect of "the horrors." It was not a plague in the true sense: it struck singly, randomly, wantonly. It jumped between planets, from one end of Occupied Space to the other, closing off the minds of victim after victim. To date we remain ignorant of the nature of the malady. An effective prophylaxis was never devised. And there was only one known cure—a man called The Healer.

The Healer made his initial public appearance at the Chesney Institute for Psychophysiologic Disorders on Largo IV under the auspices of the Interstellar Medical Corps. Intense investigative reporting by the vid services at the time revealed that a man of similar appearance (and there could have been only one then) was seen frequently about the IMC research center on Tolive.

IMC, however, has been steadfastly and frustratingly recalcitrant about releasing any information concerning its relationship with The Healer, saying only that they gave him "logistical support" as he went from planet to planet. As to whether they discovered his talent, developed his talent, or actually imbued him with his remarkable psionic powers, only IMC knows.

from *The Healer: Man & Myth*

by Emmerz Fent

IV

THE MAN STROLLS slowly along one of Chesney's wide thoroughfares, enjoying the sun. His view of the street ahead of him is suddenly blotted out by the vision of a huge, contorted face leering horribly at him. For an instant he thinks he can feel the brush of its breath on his face. Then it is gone.

He stops and blinks. Nothing like this has ever happened to him before. He tentatively scrapes a foot forward to start walking again and kicks up a cloud of—

—dust. An arid wasteland surrounds him and the sun regards him cruelly, reddening and blistering his skin. And when he feels that his blood is about to boil, the sky is suddenly darkened by the wings of a huge featherless bird which circles twice and then dives in his direction at a speed which will certainly smash them both. Closer, the cavernous beaked mouth is open and hungry. Closer, until he is—

—back on the street. The man leans against the comforting solidity of a nearby building. He is bathed in sweat and his respiration is ragged, gulping. He is afraid . . . must find a doctor. He pushes away from the building and—

—falls into a black void. But it is not a peaceful blackness. There's hunger there. He falls, tumbling in

51

eternity. A light below. As he falls nearer, the light takes shape . . . an albino worm, blind, fanged and miles long, awaits him with gaping jaws.

A scream is torn from him, yet there is no sound.

And still he falls.

V

PARD WAS PLAYING games again. The shuttle from Tarvodet had docked against the orbiting liner and as the passengers were making the transfer, he attempted to psionically influence their choice of seats.

("The guy in blue is going to sit in the third recess on the left.")

Are you reading him? Dalt asked.

("No, nudging him.")

You never give up, do you? You've been trying to work this trick for as long as I can remember.

("Yeah, but this time I think I've got it down. Watch.")

Dalt watched as the man in blue suddenly stopped before the third recess on the left, hesitated, then entered and seated himself.

"Well, congratulations," Dalt whispered aloud.

("Thank you, sir. Now watch the teenager sit in the same recess.")

The lanky young man in question ambled by the third recess on the left without so much as a glance and settled himself in the fifth on the right.

("Damn!")

What happened?

("Ah, the kid probably had his mind already made up that he wanted to sit there . . . probably does a lot of traveling and likes that seat.'')

Possible. It's also possible that the guy in blue does a lot of traveling, too, and that he just so happens to like to sit in the third recess on the left.

(''Cynicism doesn't become you, Steve.'')

Well, it's hard to be an engenue after a couple of centuries with you.

(''Then let me explain. You see, I can't make a person part his hair on the left if he prefers it parted on the right. However, if he doesn't give a damn where it's parted, I can probably get him to do it my way.'')

A slim, blond beauty in an opalescent clingsuit strolled through the port.

(''Okay, where should we make her sit?'')

I don't care.

(''Oh, yes you do. Your heart rate just increased four beats per minute and you groin is tingling.'')

I'll admit she's attractive—

(''She's more than that. She bears a remarkable resemblance to Jean, doesn't she?'')

I really hadn't noticed.

(''Come now, Steve. You know you can't lie to me. You saw the likeness immediately . . . you've never forgotten that woman.'')

And he probably never would. It was over 140 standard years since he'd left her. What started as a casual shipboard romance during the Kwashi expedition had stretched into an incredible idyll. She accepted him completely, though it had puzzled her that he'd refused disability compensation for the loss of his left hand on Kwashi. Her puzzlement was short-lived, however, and was soon replaced by astonishment when it became evident that her lover's hand was growing back. She'd heard of alien creatures who could regenerate limbs and there was talk that the Interstellar Medical Corps was experimenting with induced regeneration, but this was spontaneous!

And if the fact that the hand was regenerating was not bizarre enough, the manner in which it regenerated bordered on the surreal. No finger buds appeared; no initial primitive structures heralded the reconstruction of the severed hand. Instead, the wrist was repaired first, then the thenar and hypothenar eminences and the palm started to appear. The palm and the five metacarpals were completed before work was begun on the thumb phalanges; and the thumb, nail and all, was completed before the fingers were started. It was similar to watching a building being constructed floor by floor but with every floor completely furnished before the next one above is started. It took four standard months.

Jean accepted that—was glad, in fact, that her man had been made whole again. And then Dalt explained to her that he was no longer entirely human, that a new factor had been added, had entered through that patch of silver hair on the top of his head. He was a dual entity: one brain but two minds, and that second mind was conscious down to the cellular level.

And Jean accepted that. She might not have if it weren't for the hand which had grown back where the old one had been sliced off. No question about it: the hand was there—discolored, yes, but there nonetheless. And since that was true, then whatever else Dalt told her might also be true. So she accepted it. He was her man and she loved him and that was enough . . .

. . . until the years began to show and she watched her hair begin to thin and her skin begin to dry. The youth treatments were new then and only minimally effective. Yet all the while the man she loved remained in his prime, appearing to be not a day older than when they had met. This she could not accept. And so slowly her love began to thin, began to dry, began to crumble into resentment. And from there it was not far to desperate hatred.

So Dalt left Jean—for her sake, for the sake of her sanity. And never returned.

("I think I'll have her sit right here next to you.")

Don't bother.

("I think I should bother. You've avoided a close male-female relationship ever since you left Jean. I don't think that's—")

I really don't care what you think. Just don't play matchmaker!

("Nevertheless . . .")

The girl paused by Dalt's shoulder. Her voice was liquid. "Saving that seat for anyone?"

Dalt sighed resignedly. "No." He watched her as she settled herself across from him. She certainly did justice to the clingsuit: slim enough to keep the suit from bulging in the wrong places, full enough to fill it out and make it live up to its name. He idly wondered how Jean would have looked in one and then quickly cut off that train of thought.

"My name's Ellen Lettre."

"Steven Dalt," he replied with a mechanical nod.

A pause, then: "Where're you from, Steve?"

"Derby." Another pause, this one slightly more awkward than the first.

("Have mercy on the girl! She's just trying to make friendly conversation. Just because she looks like Jean is no reason to treat her as if she's got Nolevatol Rot!")

You're right, he thought, then spoke. "I was doing some microbial research at the university there."

She smiled and that was nice to see. "Really? That means you were connected with the bioscience department. I took Dr. Chamler's course there last year."

"Ah! The Chemistry of Schizophrenia. A classic course. Are you in psychochem?"

She nodded. "Coming back from a little field trip right now, as a matter of fact. But I don't remember seeing you around the bioscience department."

"I sort of kept pretty much to myself—very involved in the work." And this was true. Dalt and Pard had developed a joint interest in the myriad microbial lifeforms being found on the explorable planets of the human sector of the galaxy. Some of the metabolic pathways and enzyme systems were incredible and the "laws" of biological science were constantly being rearranged. Alien microbiology had become a huge field requiring years to make a beginning and decades to make a dent. Dalt and Pard had made notable contributions and published a number of respected papers.

"Dalt . . . Dalt," the girl was saying. "Yes, I believe I did hear your name mentioned around the department a few times. Funny, I'd have thought you'd be older than you are."

So would his fellow members of the bioscience department if he hadn't quit when he did. Men who had looked his age when he first came to the university were now becoming large in the waist and gray in the hair and it was time to move. Already two colleagues had asked him where he was taking his youth treatments. Fortunately, IMC Central had offered him an important research fellowship in antimicrobial therapy and he had accepted eagerly.

"You on a sabbatical from Derby?" she was asking.

"No, I quit. I'm on my way to Tolive now."

"Oh, then you're going to be working for the Interstellar Medical Corps."

"How did you know?"

"Tolive is the main research-and-development headquarters for IMC. Any scientist is assumed to be working for the group if he's headed for Tolive."

"I don't consider myself a scientist, really. Just a vagabond student of sorts, going from place to place and picking up what I can." So far, Dalt and his partner had served as an engineer on a peristellar freighter, a prospector on Tandem, a chispen fisher on Gelc, and so on, in a leisurely but determined search for knowledge and experience that spanned the human sector of the galaxy.

"Well, I'm certain you'll pick up a lot with IMC."

"You've worked for them?"

"I'm head of a psychiatric unit. My spesh is really behavior mod, but I'm trying to develop an overview of the entire field; that's why I took Chamler's course."

Dalt nodded. "Tell me something, Ellen—"

"El—"

"Okay, then: El. What's IMC like to work for? I must confess that I'm taking this job rather blindly; the offer came and I accepted with only minimal research.''

''I wouldn't work anywhere else,'' she stated flatly, and Dalt believed her. ''IMC has gathered some of the finest minds in the human galaxy together for one purpose: knowledge.''

''Knowledge for knowledge's sake has never had that much appeal for me; and frankly, that's not quite the image I'd been given about IMC. It has a rather mercenary reputation in academic circles.''

''The practical scientist and the practicing physician have limited regard for the opinions of most academicians. And I'm no exception. The IMC was started with private funds—loans, not grants—by a group of rather adventurous physicians who—''

''It was a sort of emergency squad, wasn't it?''

''At first, yes. There was always a plague of some sort somewhere and the group hopped from place to place on a fee-for-service basis. Mostly, they could render only supportive care; the pathogens and toxins encountered on the distressed planets had already been found resistant to current therapeutic measures and there was not much the group could do on such short notice, other than lend a helping hand. They came up with some innovations which they patented, but it became clear that much basic research was needed. So they set up a permanent base on Tolive and started digging.''

''With quite a bit of success, I believe. IMC is reputedly wealthy—extremely so.''

''Nobody's starving, I can say that. IMC pays well in hopes of attracting the best minds. It offers an incredible array of research resources and gives the individual a good share of the profits from his marketable discoveries. As a matter of fact, we've just leased to Teblinko Pharmaceuticals rights for production of the antitoxin for the famous Nolevatol Rot.''

Dalt was impressed. The Nolevatol Rot was the scourge of the interstellar traveler. Superficially, it resembled a mild case of tinea and was self-limiting; however, the fungus produced a neurotoxin with invariably fatal central-nervous-system effects. It was highly contagious and curable only by early discovery and immediate excision of the affected area of skin . . . until now.

"That product alone would finance the entire operation of IMC, I imagine."

El shook her head. "Not a chance. I can see you have no idea of the scope of the group. For every trail that pays off, a thousand are followed to a dead end. And they all cost money. One of our most costly fiascoes was Nathan Sebitow."

"Yes, I'd heard he'd quit."

"He was *asked* to quit. He may be the galaxy's greatest biophysicist but he's dangerous—complete disregard of safety precautions for both himself and his fellow workers. IMC gave him countless warnings but he ignored them all. He was working with some fairly dangerous radiation and so finally his funds were cut off."

"Well, it didn't take him long to find a new home, I imagine."

"No, Kamedon offered him everything he needed to continue his work within days after he supposedly 'quit' IMC."

"Kamedon . . . that's the model planet the Restructurists are pouring so much money into."

She nodded. "And Nathan Sebitow is quite a feather in its cap. He should come up with something very exciting—I just hope he doesn't kill anybody with that hard radiation he's fooling around with." She paused, then, "But getting back to the question of knowledge for knowledge's sake: I find the concept unappealing, too. IMC, however, works on the assumption that all knowledge—at least scientific knowledge—will eventually work its way into some scheme of practical value. Existence consists of intra- and extracorporeal phenomena; the more we know about those two groups, the more effective our efforts will be when we wish to remedy certain interactions between them which prove to be detrimental to a given human.''

"Spoken like a true behaviorist,'' Dalt said with a laugh.

"Sorry.'' She flushed. "I do get carried away now and again. Anyway, you see the distinction I was trying to make.''

"I see and agree. It's good to know that I'm not headed for an oversized ivory tower. But why Tolive? I mean, I've—''

"Tolive was chosen for its political and economic climate: a non-coercive government and a large, young work force. The presence of IMC and the ensuing prosperity have stabilized both the government—and I use that term only because you're an outsider—and the economy.''

"But I've heard stories about Tolive.''

"You mean that it's run by a group of sadists and fascists and anarchists and whatever other unpleasant terms you can dig up, and that if it weren't for the presence of the IMC the planet would quickly degenerate into a hell-hole, right?''

"Well, not quite so bluntly put, perhaps, but that's the impression I've been given. No specific horror stories, just vague warnings. Any of it true?''

"Don't ask me. I was born there and I'm prejudiced. But guess who else was born there, and I think you'll know what's behind the smear campaign.''

Dalt pondered a moment, baffled. Pard, with his absolute recall, came to the rescue. ("Peter LaNague was born on Tolive.'')

"LaNague!'' Dalt blurted in surprise. "Of course!''

El raised her eyebrows. "Good for you. Not too many people remember that fact.''

"But you're implying that someone is trying to smear LaNague by smearing his homeworld. That's ridiculous. Who would want to smear the author of the Federation Charter?''

"Why, the people who are trying to alter that charter: the Restructurists, of course. Tolive has been pretty much the way it is today for centuries, long before

LaNague's birth and long since his death. Only since the Restructurist movement gained momentum have the rumors and whispers started. It's the beginning of a long-range campaign; you watch—it'll get dirtier. The idea is to smear LaNague's background and thus taint his ideas, thereby casting doubt upon the integrity of his life-work: the Federation Charter."

"You must be mistaken. Besides, lies can easily be exposed."

"Lies, yes. But not rumors and inference. We of Tolive have a rather unique way of viewing existence, a view that can easily be twisted and distorted into something repulsive."

"If you're trying to worry me, you're doing an excellent job. You'd better tell me what I've gotten myself into."

Her smile was frosty. "Nobody twisted your arm, I assume? You're on your way to Tolive of your own free choice, and I think you should learn about it firsthand. And speaking of hands . . ."

Dalt noticed her gaze directed at his left hand. "Oh, you've noticed the color."

"It's hard to miss."

He examined the hand, pronating and supinating it slowly as he raised it from his lap; a yellow hand, deepening to gold in the nail beds and somewhat mottled in the palms. At the wrist, normal flesh tone resumed along a sharp line of demarcation. Anthon's sword had been sharp and had cut clean.

"I had a chemical accident a few years back which left my hand permanently stained."

El's brow furrowed as she considered this.

("Careful, Steve,") Pard warned. ("This gal's connected with the medical profession and may not fall for that old story.")

"That can easily be remedied," El said after a pause. "I know a few cosmetic surgeons on Tolive—"

Dalt shook his head and cut her off. "Thanks, no. I leave it this color to remind me to be more careful in the future. I could have been killed."

("Go on! Persist in your stubbornness! For almost
two centuries now you've refused to allow me to correct
that unsightly pigmentation. It was my fault, I admit.
I'd never overseen the reconstruction of an appendage
before and I—")

*I know, I know! You made an error in the melanin
deposition. We've been over this more times than I care
to remember.*

("And I can correct it if you'll just let me! You know
I can't stand the thought of our having one yellow hand.
It grates on me.")

*That's because you're an obsessive-compulsive per-
sonality.*

("Hah! That's merely a term used by slobs to deni-
grate perfectionists!")

El was now eyeing the gray patch of hair on the top of
his head. "Is that, too, the result of an accident?"

"A terrible accident." He nodded gravely.

("No fair! I can't defend myself!")

She leaned back and appraised him. "A golden hand,
a crown of silver hair, and a rather large flamestone
hanging from your neck—you cut quite a figure, Steven
Dalt." El was frankly interested.

Dalt fingered the jewel at his throat and pretended
not to notice. "This little rock is a memento of a previous and far more hazardous form of employment. I
keep it for sentimental reasons only."

"You have lots of color for a microbiologist," she
was saying, and her smile was very warm now, "and I
think you'll make a few waves at IMC."

A few days later they sat in the lounge of the orbit station and watched Tolive swirl below them as they sipped
drinks and waited for the shuttle to arrive. A portly man
in a blue jumper drifted by and paused to share the view
with them.

"Beautiful, isn't it?" he said, and they replied with
nods. "I don't know what it is, but every time I get in
front of a view like this, I feel so insignificant. Don't
you?"

El ignored the question and posed one of her own.

"You aren't from Tolive, are you?" It was actually a statement.

"No, I'm on my way to Neeka. Have to lay over in orbit here to make a connecting jump. Never been down there," he said, nodding at the globe below. "But how come you sound so sure?"

"Because no one from 'down there' would ever say what you said," El replied, and promptly lost interest in the conversation. The portly man paused, shrugged, and then drifted off.

"What was that all about?" Dalt asked. "What did he say that was so un-Tolivian?"

"As I told you before, we have a different way of looking at things. The human race developed on a tiny planet a good many light-years away and devised a technology that allows us to sit in orbit above a once-alien planet and comfortably sip intoxicants while awaiting a ship to take us down. As a member of that race, I assure you, I feel anything but insignificant."

Dalt glanced after the man who had initiated the discussion and noticed him stagger as he walked away. He widened his stance as if to steady himself and stood blinking at nothing, beads of sweat dropping from his face and darkening the blue of his jumper. Suddenly he spun with outstretched arms, and with a face contorted with horror, began to scream incoherently.

El bolted from her seat without a word and dug a microsyringe from her hip pouch as she strode toward the man, who had by now collapsed into a blubbering, whimpering puddle of fear. She placed the ovid device on the skin on the lateral aspect of his neck and squeezed.

"He'll quiet down in a minute," she told a concerned steward as he rushed up. "Send him down to IMC Central on the next shuttle for emergency admission to Section Blue." The steward nodded obediently, relieved that someone seemed to feel that things were under control. And sure enough, by the time two fellow workers had arrived, the portly man was quiet, although still racked with sobs.

"What the hell happened to him?" Dalt asked over El's shoulder as the man was carried to a berth in the rear.

"A bad case of the horrors," she replied.

"No, I'm serious."

"So am I. It's been happening all over the human sector of the galaxy, just like that: men, women, all ages; they go into an acute, unremitting psychotic state. They are biochemically normal and usually have unremarkable premorbid medical histories. They've been popping up for the past decade in a completely random fashion and there doesn't seem to be a damn thing we can do about them," she said with a set jaw, and it was obvious that she resented being helpless in any situation, especially a medical one.

Dalt gazed at El and felt the heaviness begin. She was a remarkable woman, very intelligent, very opinionated, and so very much like Jean in appearance; but she was also very mortal. Dalt had resisted the relationship she was obviously trying to initiate and every time he weakened he merely had to recall Jean's hate-contorted face when he had deserted her.

I think we ought to get out of microbiology, he told Pard as his eyes lingered on El.

("And into what?")

How about life prolongation?

("Not that again!")

Yes! Only this time we'll be working at IMC Central with some of the greatest scientific minds in the galaxy.

("The greatest minds in the galaxy have always worked on that problem, and every 'major breakthrough' and 'new hope' has turned out to be a dead end. Human cells reach a certain level of specialization and then lose their ability to reproduce. Under optimum conditions, a century is all they'll last; after that the DNA gets sloppy and consequently the RNA gets even sloppier. What follows is enzyme breakdown, toxic overload, and finally death. Why this happens, no one knows—and that includes me, since my consciousness doesn't reach to the molecular level—and from recent literature, it doesn't seem likely that anyone'll know in the near future.")

But we have a unique contribution to make—

("You think I haven't investigated it on my own, if not for any other reason than to provide you with a human companion of some permanence? It's no fun, you know, when you go into those periods of black despair.")

I guess not. He paused. *I think one's on its way.*

("I know. The metabolic warning flags are already up. Look: why not take up with this woman? You both find each other attractive and I think it will be good for you.")

Will it be good for me when she grows into a bitter old woman while I stay young?

("What makes you think she'll want you around that long?") Pard jibed.

Dalt had no answer for that one.

The shuttle trip was uneventful and when El offered to drive him from the spaceport to his hotel, Dalt reluctantly accepted. His feelings were in a turmoil, wanting to be simultaneously as close to and as far from this woman as possible. So to keep the conversation safe and light, he made a comment about the lack of flitters in the air.

"We're pretty much in the ground-car stage, although one of the car factories is reportedly gearing for flitter production. It'll be nice to get one at a reasonable price; the only ones on Tolive now were shipped via interstellar freight and *that* is expensive!"

She pulled her car alongside a booth outside the spaceport perimeter, fished out a card, and stuck it into a slot. The card disappeared for a second or two and then the booth spit it out. El retrieved it, sealed her bubble, and pulled away.

"What was that all about?"

"Toll."

Dalt was incredulous. "You mean you actually have toll roads on this planet?"

She nodded. "But not for long . . . not if we get a good supply of flitters."

"Even so, the roads belong to everybody—"

"No, they belong to those who built them."

"But taxes—"

"You think roads should be built with tax money?" El asked with a penetrating glance. "I use this road maybe once or twice a year; why should I pay anything for it the rest of the time? A group of men got together and built this road and they charge me every time I use it. What's wrong with that?"

"Nothing, except you've got to fork over money every time you make a turn."

"Not necessarily. Members of a given community usually get together and pool their money for local streets, build them, and leave them at that; and business areas provide roads gratis for the obvious reason. As a matter of fact, a couple of our big corporations have built roads and donated them to the public—the roads are, of course, named after the companies and thus act as continuous publicity agents."

"Sounds like a lot of trouble to me. It'd be a lot simpler if you just made everyone ante up and—"

"Not on this planet it wouldn't be. You don't *make* Tolivians do anything. It would take a physical threat to make me pay for a road that I'll never use. And we tend to frown on the use of physical force here."

"A pacifist society, huh?"

"Pacifist may not be—" she began, and then swerved sharply to make an exit ramp. "Sorry," she said with a quick, wry grin. "I forgot I was dropping you off at the hotel."

Dalt let the conversation lapse and stared out his side of the bubble at the Tolivian landscape. Nothing remarkable there: a few squat trees resembling conifers scattered in clumps here and there around the plain, coarse grass, a mountain range rising in the distance.

"Not exactly a lush garden-world," he muttered after a while.

"No, this is the arid zone. Tolive's axis has little deviation relative to its primary, and its orbit is only mildly ellipsoid. So whatever the weather is wherever you happen to be, that's probably what it'll be like for most of the year. Most of our agriculture is in the northern hemisphere; industry keeps pretty much to the south and usually within short call of the spaceports."

"You sound like a chamber-of-commerce report," Dalt remarked with a smile.

"I'm proud of my world." El did not smile.

Suddenly, there was a city crouched on the road ahead, waiting for them. Dalt had spent too much time on Derby of late and had become accustomed to cities with soaring profiles. And that's how the cities on his homeworld of Friendly had been. But this pancake of one-and two-story buildings was apparently the Tolivian idea of a city.

SPOONERVILLE said a sign in interworld characters. POP: 78,000. They sped by rows of gaily colored houses, most standing alone, some interconnected. And then there were warehouses and shops and restaurants and such. The hotel stood out among its neighboring buildings, stretching a full four stories into the air.

"Not exactly the Centauri Hilton," Dalt remarked as the car jolted to a halt before the front entrance.

"Tolive doesn't have much to offer in the way of tourism. This place obviously serves Spoonerville's needs, 'cause if there was much of an overflow somebody'd have built another." She paused, caught his eyes, and held them. "I've got a lovely little place out on the plain that'll accommodate two very nicely, and the sunsets are incredible."

Dalt tried to smile. He liked this woman, and the invitation, which promised more than sunsets, was his for the taking. "Thanks, El. I'd like to take you up on that offer sometime, but not now. I'll try to see you at IMC tomorrow after my meeting with Dr. Webst."

"Okay." She sighed as he stepped out of the car. "Good luck." Without another word she sealed the bubble and was off.

("You know what they say about hell and fury and

scorned women,'') Pard remarked.

Yeah, I know, but I don't think she's like that . . . got too good a head on her shoulders to react so primitively.

Dalt's reserved room was ready for him and his luggage was expected to arrive momentarily from the spaceport. He walked over to the window which had been left opaque, flipped a switch, and made the entire outer wall transparent. It was 18.75 in a twenty-seven-hour day—that would take some getting used to after years of living with Derby's twenty-two-hour day—and the sunset was an orange explosion behind the hills. It probably looked even better from El's place on the plains.

(''But you turned her down,'') Pard said, catching the thought. (''Well, what are we going to do with ourselves tonight? Shall we go out and see what the members of this throbbing metropolis do to entertain themselves?'')

Dalt squatted down by the window with his back against the wall. ''I think I'll just stay here and watch for a while. Why don't you just go away,'' he muttered aloud.

(''I can't very well leave . . .'')

''You know what I mean!''

(''Yes, I know what you mean. We go through this every time we have to uproot ourselves because your associates start giving you funny looks. You start mooning over Jean—'')

''I do *not* moon over her!''

(''Call it what you will, you mope around like a Lentemian crench that's lost its calf. But it's really not Jean. She's got nothing to do with these mood swings; she's dead and gone and you've long since accepted that. What's really bothering you is your own immortality. You refuse to let people know that you will not grow old with the years as they do—'')

''I don't want to be a freak and I don't want that kind of notoriety. Before you know it, someone will come looking for the 'secret' of my longevity and will stop at nothing to get it. I can do very well without that, thank you.''

("Fine. Those are good reasons, excellent reasons for wanting to pass yourself off as a mortal among mortals. That's the only way we'll ever really get to do what we want to do. But that's only on the surface. Inside you must come to grips with the fact that you cannot *live* as a mortal. You haven't the luxury of ascribing an infinite span to a relationship, as do many mortals, for 'the end of time' to them is the same as the end of life, which is all too finite. In your case, however, 'the end of time' may occur with you there watching it. So, until you can find yourself another immortal as a companion, you'll just have to be satisfied with relatively short-term relationships and cease acting so resentful of the fact that you won't be dying in a few decades like all your friends.")

"Sometimes I wish I *could* die."

("Now, we both know that you don't mean that, and even if you were sincere, I wouldn't allow it.")

Go away, Pard!

("I'm gone.")

And he was. With Pard tucked away in some far corner of his brain—probably working on some obscure philosophical problem or remote mathematical abstraction—Dalt was finally alone.

Alone. That was the key to these periodic black depressions. He was all right once he had established an identity on a new world, made a few friends, and put himself to work on whatever it was he wanted to do at that particular time in his life. He could thus delude himself into a sense of belonging that lasted a few decades, and then it began to happen: the curious stares, the probing questions. Soon he'd find himself on an interstellar liner again, between worlds, between lives. The sense of rootlessness would begin to weigh heavily upon him.

Culturally, too, he was an outsider. There was no interstellar human culture as yet to speak of; each planet was developing its own traditions and becoming proud of them. No one could really feel at home on any world except one's own, and so the faux pas of an off-worlder was well tolerated in the hope of receiving the same consideration after a similar blunder on his homeworld. Dalt was thus unconcerned about any anachronisms in his behavior, and with the bits and pieces he was taking with him from every world he lived on, he was fast becoming the only representative of a true interstellar human culture.

Which meant that no world was actually *home*—only on interstellar liners did he feel even the slightest hint of belonging. Even Friendly, his birth world, had treated him as an off-worlder, and only with great difficulty did he manage to find a trace or two of the familiar in his own hometown during a recent and very discouraging sentimental journey.

Pard was right, of course. He was almost always right. Dalt couldn't have it both ways, couldn't be an immortal and retain a mortal's scope. He'd have to broaden his view of existence and learn to think on a grander scale. He was still a man and would have to live among other men, but he would have to develop an immortal's perspective in regard to time, something he had as yet been unable and/or unwilling to do. Time set him apart from other men and had to be reckoned with. Until now he had been living a lot of little lives, one after the other, separate, distinct. Yet they were all his, and he had to find a way to fuse them into a single entity. He'd work on it. No hurry . . . there was plenty of time—

There was that word again. He wondered when he would end. Or *if* he would end. Would the moment ever come when he'd want to stop living? And would he be allowed to do so? Pard's earlier statement had made him uneasy. They shared a body and thus an existence, as the result of an accident. What if one partner decided he wanted out? It would never be Pard—his intellectual appetite was insatiable. No, if anyone would ever want to call it quits, it would be Dalt. And Pard would forbid it. Such a situation appeared ludicrous on the surface but might very well come to be, millennia hence. How would they resolve it? Would Pard find a way to grant

Dalt's wish by somehow strangling his mind, thereby granting his death wish—for in Pard's philosophy, the mind is life and life is the mind—and leaving Pard as sole tenant of the body?

Dalt shuddered. Pard's ethics would, of course, prevent him from doing such a thing unless Dalt absolutely demanded it. But still it was hardly a comforting thought. Even in the dark fog of depression that enveloped him tonight, Dalt realized that he loved life and living very much. Planning to make the most of tomorrow and every subsequent tomorrow, he drifted off to sleep as the second of Tolive's three moons bobbed above the horizon.

VI

A SOMEWHAT HARRIED Steven Dalt managed to arrive at the administrative offices of IMC in time for his 09.5 appointment with Dr. Webst. His back ached as he took a seat in the waiting room, and he realized he was hungry.

A bad morning so far—if this was any indication of how the rest of the day was going to be, he decided he'd be better off returning to the hotel, crawling into bed, and spending it in the fetal position. He'd awakened late and cramped in that corner by the window, with his baggage sitting inside the door. He'd had to rummage through it to find a presentable outfit and then rush down to the lobby and find a taxi to take him to the IMC administration building. He did not want to keep Dr. Webst waiting. Dalt seemed to be placing greater and greater importance on punctuality lately. Perhaps, he mused, the more aware he became of his own time-lessness, the more conscious he became of the value of another man's time.

("Well, what'll it be?") Pard asked suddenly.

Welcome back.

("I should be saying that to you. Once again: What'll it be?")

What are you talking about?

("Us. Are we sticking with the microbes or do we go

73

into gerontology or what?'')

I'm not sure. Maybe we won't stay here at all. They hired us for antimicrobial research and may not want us for anything else. But I think I've had enough of microbes for now.

(''I must agree. But what shall we try next?'')

I haven't given it too much thought yet—

(''Well, get thinking. We'll be seeing Dr. Webst in a moment and we'd better have something to tell him.'')

Why don't we just improvise?

Pard seemed to hesitate, then, (''Okay, but let's be as honest as possible with him, 'cause we start getting paid as of this morning.'')

So, a few credits won't break IMC.

(''It would be unethical to accept payment for nothing.'')

Your rigidity wears on me after a while, Pard.

(''Value received for value given—don't forget it.'')

Okay, okay, okay.

The door to Dr. Webst's office dilated and a tall, fair young man with an aquiline profile stepped through. He glanced at Dalt, who was the room's only occupant, paused, then walked over and extended his hand. ''Dr. Dalt?''

''The 'Dalt' part is correct, but I have no doctorate.'' Actually, this was untrue; he held two doctorates in separate fields but both had been granted a number of lives ago.

''*Mister* Dalt, then. I'm Dr. Webst.'' They performed the ancient human ritual known as the handshake and Dalt liked Webst's firm grip.

''I thought you'd be older, Doctor,'' Dalt said as they entered Webst's sparsely appointed office.

Webst smiled. ''That's funny . . . I was expecting an older man, too. That paper you published a year ago on Dasein II fever and the multiple pathogens involved was a brilliant piece of work; there was an aura of age and experience about it.''

''Are you in infectious diseases?'' Dalt asked quickly, anxious to change the subject.

"No, psych is my field."

"Really? I made part of the trip from Derby in the company of Ellen Lettre. Know her?"

"Of course. Our department has high hopes for Dr. Lettre—an extremely intelligent woman." He paused at his desk and flashed a rapid series of memos across his viewer. "Before I forget, I got a note from personnel about your forms. Most of them are incomplete and they'd like to see you sometime today."

Dalt nodded. "Okay, I'll see if I can make it this afternoon." This was often a problem—personal history. He had changed his name a couple of times but preferred to be known as Steven Dalt. Usually he went from one field of endeavor to another totally unrelated to the first and thus obviated the need for references; he would start at the bottom as he had at the university on Derby, and with Pard as his partner, it wouldn't be long before the higher-ups realized they had a boy genius among them. Or, he'd go into a risky field such as chispen fishing on Gelc, where the only requirement for employment was the guts to go out on the nets . . . and no questions asked.

As for the IMC personnel department—he had paid a records official on Derby a handsome bribe to rig some documents to make him appear to be a native of the planet. He'd been purposely vague and careless with the IMC applications in order to stall off any inquiries until all was ready. All he could do now was hope.

"Question," Dalt said. Webst looked up. "Why a psychiatrist to meet me rather than someone from the microbiology department?"

"Protocol, I guess. Dr. Hyne is head of the micro department but he's on vacation. It's customary to have an important new man—and you fall into that category —welcomed by a departmental head. And I'm head of psych."

"I see," Dalt nodded. "But when do I—"

Webst's phone buzzed. "Yes?" The word activated the screen and a technician's face appeared.

"Private message, Doctor."

Webst picked up the earpiece and swung the screen face away from Dalt. "Go ahead." He listened, nodded, said, "I'll be right over," and hung up.

"Have you had breakfast yet?" he asked Dalt, whose headshake left little doubt about the current state of his stomach. "Okay, why don't you make yourself at home at that table behind you and punch in an order. I've got to go check out some equipment—should only take me a few minutes. Relax and enjoy the meal; we have an excellent commissary and the local hens lay delicious eggs." He gave a short wave and was gone.

("May the god of empty stomachs bless and keep him!") Pard remarked as Dalt punched in an order. ("No dinner last night and no breakfast this morning —very careless.")

Dalt waited hungrily. *Couldn't be helped.*

("I like Webst,") Pard said as a steaming tray popped out of a slot in the wall. ("He seems rather unpretentious and it would be easy for a young man in such a high position to be otherwise.")

I didn't notice either way. Dalt began to eat with gusto.

("That's the nice part—he doesn't make a show of his unpretentiousness. It seemed very natural for him to personally bring you in from the waiting room, didn't it? But think: Most departmental heads would prefer to have the receptionist open the door and let you come to them. This man made an effort to make you feel at home.")

Maybe he just hasn't been a head long enough and doesn't know how to act like one.

("I have a feeling, Steve, that Dr. Webst is at the top of his field and knows it and can act any way he damn well pleases.")

Webst returned then, appearing preoccupied. He went directly to his desk, seated himself, and stared at Dalt for a long moment with a puzzled expression playing over his face.

"What's the matter?" Dalt asked, finally.

"Hmmm?" He shook himself. "Oh, nothing. A

technical problem . . . I think.'' He paused. ''Tell you what: Everybody over in microbiology is rather tied up today—why don't you come with me over to psychiatry and I'll show you around. I know you're anxious to get to see micro—''

(''Not really,'') Pard interjected.

''—but at least this way you can start to get a feel for IMC.''

Dalt shrugged. ''Fine with me. Lead the way.''

Webst seemed very pleased with Dalt's acquiescence and ushered him out a rear door to a small carport.

(''He's lying to us, Steve.'')

I had that feeling, too. You think we're in trouble?

(''I doubt it. He's such a terrible liar, it's unlikely that he's had much practice at it. He just wants to get us over to the psych department, so let's play along and see what he has in mind. This just may lead to a chance to get out of microbes and into another field. Can you dredge up any interest in mental illness?'')

Not a particularly overwhelming amount.

(''Well, start asking questions anyway. Show a little interest!'')

Yessir!

''—nice weather, so I think we'll take the scenic tour,'' Webst was saying. ''When it rains, which isn't that often, we have a tunnel system you can use. A dome was planned initially but the weather proved to be so uniform that no one could justify the expense.''

The small ground car glided out over the path and the combination of warm sunlight, a cool breeze, through the open cab, and a full belly threatened to put Dalt to sleep. At a leisurely pace they passed formations of low buildings, clean and graceful, with intricate gardens scattered among them.

(''Questions, Steve,'') Pard prompted.

Right. ''Tell me, Doctor—if I may be so bold—what sort of astronomical sum did IMC have to pay for such a huge tract of land so close to the center of town?''

Webst smiled. ''You forget that IMC was here before you and I were born—''

("Speak for yourself, sir.")

"—and the town was only a village at the time Central was started. Spoonerville, in fact, grew up around IMC."

"Well, it's beautiful, I must say."

"Thank you. We're proud of it."

Dalt drank in a passing garden, then asked, "What's going on in psychiatry these days? I thought mental illness was virtually a thing of the past. You have the enzymes and—"

"The enzymes only *control* schizophrenia—much the same as insulin controlled diabetics before beta-cell grafts. There's no cure as yet and I don't foresee one for quite some time." His voice lapsed unconsciously into a lecture tone. "Everyone thought a cure was imminent when Schimmelpenninck isolated the enzyme-substrate chains in the limbic system of the brain. But that was only the beginning. Different types and degrees of schizophrenia occur with breaks at different loci along the chains but environmental history appears to be equally important."

Webst paused as the car rounded a corner and had to wait for an automatic gate to slide open. Then they were in an octagonal courtyard with people scattered here and there, in groups or alone, talking or soaking up the sun.

"These are our ambulatory patients," he replied to Dalt's questioning glance. "We give them as much freedom as possible, but we also try to keep them from wandering off. They're all harmless and they're all here voluntarily." He cleared his throat. "But where was I? . . . Oh, yes. So it all boils down to a delicate balance between chemistry, intellect, and environment. If the individual has learned how to handle stress, he can often minimize the psychotic effects of a major break in the enzyme chains. If he hasn't, however, even a minor break at the terminus of a chain can throw his mind off the deep end."

He gave a short laugh. "But we still really don't know what we're talking about when we say *mind*. We can improve its function and grasp of reality with our drugs and teaching techniques, but it remains a construct that defies quantitative analysis.''

He guided the vehicle into a slot next to a large blue building and stepped out. ''And then, of course, there are the chemonegative psychotics—all their enzyme chains seem to be intact but they are completely divorced from reality. Victims of the so-called 'horrors.' They're the one's we're working on here in Big Blue, where we keep our intractable patients,'' Webst said as he passed his hand over a plate set in the doorframe. Silently, the first of the double doors slid open and waited for them to enter, and it was not until the first was completely secure in its closed position that the second began to move.

''Are they dangerous in here?'' Dalt asked uneasily.

''Only to themselves. These patients are totally cut off from reality and anything could happen to them if they got loose.''

''But what's wrong with them? I saw a man go into one of these fits on the orbit station.''

Webst twisted his mouth to the side. ''Unfortunately, these aren't 'fits' that come and go. The victim gets hit with whatever it is that hits him, screams hysterically, and spends the rest of his life—at least we assume so, although the first recorded case was only ten years ago—cut off from the rest of the world. Cases are popping up on every planet in the Federation. It's even rumored that the Tarks are having problems with it. We need a breakthrough.''

Webst paused, then said, ''Let's look in here.'' He opened a door marked 12 and allowed Dalt to precede him into the room. It was a nicely appointed affair with a bed, two chairs, and indirect lighting. And it was empty, or at least Dalt thought it was until Webst directed his attentions to a corner behind one of the chairs. A young girl of no more than eighteen years crouched there in a shivering state of abject terror.

''First name, Sally,'' Webst intoned. ''We dubbed her that. Last name: Ragna—that's the planet on which she was found. A typical 'horrors' case: We've had her for one and a half standard years and we haven't been able to put even a chink into that wall of terror.''

Webst went to a plate in the wall by the door and waved his hand across it. "This is Dr. Webst. I'm in room twelve with Mr. Dalt."

"Thank you, Doctor," said a male voice. *"Would you mind stepping down the hall a minute?"*

"Not at all," he replied, and turned to Dalt. "Why don't you stay here and try to talk to Sally while I see what they want. She's perfectly harmless, wouldn't—couldn't—hurt anyone or anything, and that's the crux of her problem. We've normalized her enzymes and have tried every psychotropic agent known to break her shell, with no results. We've even gone so far as to reinstitute the ancient methods of electroconvulsive therapy and insulin shock." He sighed. "Nothing. So try to talk to her and see what we're up against."

With Webst gone, Dalt turned his attention to the girl.

("Pitiful, isn't it?") Pard said.

Dalt did not reply. He was staring at a girl who must have been attractive once; her face now wore a ravaged, hunted expression that had caused seemingly permanent furrows in her skin; her eyes, when not squeezed shut, were opened wide and darting in all directions. Her arms were clasped around her knees, which were drawn up to her chest, and her hands gripped each other with white-knuckled intensity.

This could be very interesting, Dalt told Pard at last.

("It certainly could. I think it could also be interesting to know what Dr. Webst is up to. He was obviously stalling for time when he left us here.")

Maybe he wants us for his department.

("Highly unlikely. To the best of his knowledge, we are eminently unqualified in this field.")

"Hello, Sally," Dalt said.

No reaction.

"Do you hear me, Sally?"

No reaction.

He waved his hand before her eyes.

No reaction.

He clapped his hands loudly and without warning by her left ear.

No reaction.

He put his hands on her shoulders and shook her gently but firmly.

No reaction. Not an extra blink, not a change in expression, not a sound, not the slightest hint of voluntary movement.

Dalt rose to his feet and turned to find Dr. Webst standing in the doorway staring at him.

"Something wrong, Doctor?" Again, he wore the preoccupied, puzzled expression that did not seem to be at home on his face.

"I don't think so," he replied slowly. "Something may be very right, as a matter of fact. But I'll have to look into it a little more." He looked frustrated. "Would you mind going over to personnel for now and straightening out your papers while I try to straighten out a few things over here? I know what you're thinking . . . but IMC is really much better organized than I've demonstrated it to be. It's just that we've had some strange occurrences this morning that I'll explain to you later. For the moment, however, I'm going to be tied up."

Dalt had no desire to talk to the personnel department. On an impulse, he asked, "Is Ellen around?"

Webst brightened immediately. "Dr. Lettre? Yes, she's in the next building." He guided Dalt back to the entrance and pointed to a red building on the other side of the garden, perhaps twenty meters away. "Her office is right inside the far door. I'm sure she'll be glad to show you around her section, and I'll contact you there later." He passed his hand over the doorplate and the inner door began to move.

("Nice security system,") Pard said as they strolled past the lolling patients. ("The intercoms and the door-locks are all cued to the palms of authorized personnel. Patients stay where you put them.")

Unless of course someone gets violent and decides that the quickest way to freedom is to cut off someone's authorized hand and waltz right out of the complex.

("Your sense of humor eludes me at times . . . but let's get to more-pressing matters.")

Such as?

("Such as Webst. At first he lied to get us over to the psychiatry units; now he seems anxious to get rid of us and made up some lame excuses to do so. I'd very much like to know what he's up to.")

Maybe he's just inefficient and disorganized.

("I assure you, Steve, that man is anything but inefficient. He's obviously puzzled by something and we seem to be implicated.")

He did, however, promise to explain it all to us later.

("Correct. Hopefully, he'll keep that promise.")

The door Webst had pointed out opened easily at Dalt's touch and did not lock after him. He concluded that there must not be any patients quartered in this area of the building. On a door to his left was a brass plate engraved DR. ELLEN H. LETTRE. He knocked.

"Come in," said a familiar voice. El looked almost as beautiful in a gray smock as she had in her clingsuit aboard ship.

"Hasn't that dictation come through yet?" she asked without looking up. "It's been almost ten minutes."

"I'm sure it'll be along soon," Dalt said.

El's head snapped up and she gave him a smile that he didn't feel he deserved after his cool treatment of her the night before. "How'd you get here?" she asked brightly.

"Dr. Webst showed me the way."

"You know him?"

"Since this morning."

"Oh? I thought you were going to be with the microbi—"

Dalt held up his hand. "It's a long story which I don't fully understand myself, but I'm here and you said you'd show me around your unit someday. So?"

"Okay. I was about to take a break anyway." She

took him on a leisurely tour of her wing of the building where various behaviorist principles were being put to work on the rehabilitation of schizophrenics who had successfully responded to medical management. Dalt's stomach was starting to rumble again as they returned to her office.

"Can I buy you lunch?"

"You sure you want to get that involved?" she said with a sidelong glance.

"Okay," Dalt laughed, "I deserved that. But how about it? You've got to eat somewhere."

She smiled. "I'd love to have you buy me lunch, but first I've got to catch up on a few things—that 'break' I just took was well over an hour long." She thought for a minute. "There's a place on the square—"

"You actually have a town square?" Dalt exclaimed.

"It's a tradition on Tolive; just about every town has one. The town square is one of the very few instances of common ownership on the planet. It is used for public discussion and . . . uh . . . other matters of public concern."

"Sounds like a quaint locale for a restaurant. Should be nice."

"It is. Why don't you meet me there at 13.0. You can familiarize yourself with the square and maybe catch a little of the flavor of Tolive." The square was near the IMC complex and she told him how to get there, then called an orderly to drive him out of the maze of buildings to the front entrance.

A cool breeze offset the warmth of the sun as he walked and when he compared the vaguely remembered cab trip of the morning to the route El had given him, he realized that his hotel was right off the square. He scrutinized his fellow pedestrians in an effort to discern a fashion trend but couldn't find one. Men wore everything from briefs to business jumpers; women could be seen in everything from saris through clingsuits to near-nude.

Shops began to proliferate along the street and Dalt sensed he was nearing the square. A sign caught his eye:

LIN'S LIT in large letters, and below, at about a quarter of the size above, *For the Discerning Viewer.*

("There's plenty of time before your lunch date. Let's see what they sell on Tolive—you can learn a lot about a culture's intellectual climate from its literature.")

All right. Let's see.

They should have been prepared for what was inside by the card on the door: "Please be advised that the material sold within is considered by certain people to be obscene—you might be one of those people."

Inside they found a huge collection of photos, holos, telestories, vid cassettes, etc., most devoted to sexual activity. Categories ranged from human & human, through human & alien animal, to human & alien plant. And then the material took a sick turn.

I'm leaving, Dalt told Pard.

("Wait a minute. It's just starting to get interesting.")

Not for me. I've had enough.

("Immortals aren't supposed to be squeamish.")

Well, it'll be a couple more centuries before I can stomach some of this junk. So much for Tolive's cultural climate!

And out they went to the street again. Half a block on, they came to the square, which was actually round. It was more like a huge traffic circle with the circumference rimmed by shops and small business offices; inside the circle was a park with grass and trees and amusement areas for children. A large white structure was set at its hub; from Dalt's vantage point it appeared to be some sort of monument or oversized art object in the ancient abstract mode.

He wandered into a clothing store and was tempted to make some purchases until he remembered that he had no credit on Tolive as yet, so he contented himself with watching others do the buying. He watched a grossly overweight woman step onto a fitting platform, punch in a style, fabric weight and color code, and then wait for the measuring sensors to rise out of the floor. A *beep* announced that her order was being processed and she stepped down and took a seat by the wall to wait for the piece she had ordered to be custommade to her specifications.

A neighboring shop sold pharmaceuticals and Dalt browsed through aimlessly until he heard a fellow shopper ask for five hundred-milligram doses of Zemmelar, the trade name for a powerful hallucinogenic narcotic.

"You sure you know what you're getting into?" the man behind the counter asked.

The customer nodded. "I use it regularly."

The counterman sighed, took the customer's credit slips, and punched out the order. Five cylindrical packages popped onto the counter. "You're on your own," he told the man who pocketed the order and hurried away.

Glancing at Dalt, the counterman burst out laughing, then held up his hand as Dalt turned to leave. "I'm sorry, sir, but by the expression on your face a moment ago, you must be an off-worlder."

"What's that supposed to mean?"

"It means that you think you just witnessed a very bold illegal transaction."

"Well, didn't I? That drug is reserved for terminal cases, is it not?"

"That's what it was developed for," the man replied. "Supposed to block out all bodily sensations and accentuate the patient's most pleasant fantasies. When I'm ready to go, I hope somebody will have the good sense to shoot some of it into me."

"But that man said he uses it regularly."

"Yeah. He's an addict I guess. Probably new in town . . . never seen him before."

"But that drug is illegal!"

"That's how I know you're an off-worlder. You see —there are no illegal drugs on Tolive."

"That can't be true!"

"I assure you, sir, it is. Anything in particular you'd like to order?"

"No," Dalt said, turning slowly and walking away. "Nothing, thanks."

This place will take some getting used to, he told Pard as they crossed the street to the park and took a seat on the grass beneath one of the native conifers.

("Yes. Apparently they do not have the usual taboos that most of humanity carried with it from Earth during the splinter-world period.)

I think I like some of those taboos. Some of the stuff in that first shop was positively degrading. And as for making it possible for anybody with a few credits to become a Zem addict . . . I don't like it.

("But you must admit that this appears to be a rather genteel populace. Despite the lack of a few taboos traditional to human culture, they all seem quite civilized so far. Admit it.")

All right, I admit it.

Dalt glanced across the park and noticed that there were a number of people on the white monument. Letters, illegible from this distance, had been illuminated on a dark patch near the monument's apex. As he watched, a cylinder arose from the platform and extended what appeared to be a stiff, single-jointed appendage with some sort of thong streaming from the end. A shirtless young man was brought to the platform. There was some milling around, and then his arms were fastened to an abutment.

The one-armed machine began to whip him across his bare back.

VII

"FINISH THAT DRINK before we talk," El said.

"There's really not much to talk about," Dalt replied curtly. "I'm getting off this planet as soon as I can find a ship to take me."

They drank in silence amid the clatter and chatter of a busy restaurant, and Dalt's thoughts were irresistibly drawn back to that incredible scene in the park just as he himself had been irresistibly drawn across the grass for a closer look, to try to find some evidence that it was all a hoax. But the man's cries of pain and the rising welts on his back left little doubt. No one else in the park appeared to take much notice; some paused to look at the sign that overhung the tableau, then idly strolled on.

Dalt, too, looked at the sign:

> A. Nelso
> *Accused* of theft of
> private ground car on
> 9-6.
> *Convicted* of same on
> 9-20. Appeal denied.
> *Sentence* of public
> punishment to 0.6 Gomler
> units to be administered
> on 9-24.

The whipping stopped and the sign flashed blank. The man was released from the pillory and helped from the platform. Dalt was trying to decide whether the tears in the youth's eyes were from pain or humiliation, when a young, auburn-haired woman of about thirty years ascended the platform. She wore a harness of sorts that covered her breasts and abdomen but left her back exposed. As attendants locked her to the pillory, the sign came to life again:

> H. T. Hammet
> *Accused* of theft of
> miniature vid set from
> retail store on 9–8.
> *Convicted* of same on
> 9–22. Appeal denied.
> *Sentence* of public
> punishment to 0.2 Gomler
> units to be administered
> on 9–24.

The cylinder raised the lash, swung its arm, and the woman winced and bit her lower lip. Dalt spun and lurched away.

("Barbaric!") Pard said when they had crossed the street and were back among the storefronts.

What? No remarks about being squeamish?

("Holograms of deviant sexual behavior posed for by volunteers are quite different from public floggings. How can supposedly civilized people allow such stone-age brutality to go on?")

I don't know and I don't care. Tolive has just lost a prospective citizen.

A familiar figure suddenly caught his eye. It was El.

"Hi!" she said breathlessly. "Sorry I'm late."

"I didn't notice," he said coldly. "I was too busy watching that atavistic display in the park."

She grabbed his arm. "C'mon. Let's eat."

"I assure you, I'm not hungry."

"Then at least have a drink and we'll talk." She tugged on his arm.

("Might as well, Steve. I'd be interested in hearing how she's going to defend public floggings.")

Noting a restaurant sign behind him, Dalt shrugged and started for the entrance.

"Not there," El said. "They lost their sticker last week. We'll go to Logue's—it's about a quarter-way around."

El made no attempt at conversation as she led him around to the restaurant she wanted. During the walk, Dalt allowed his eyes to stray toward the park only once. Not a word was spoken between them until they were seated inside with drinks before them. Logue's modest furnishings and low lighting were offset by its extravagant employment of human waiters.

It was not until the waiter had brought Dalt his second drink that he finally broke the silence.

"You wanted me to see those floggings, didn't you," he said, holding her eyes. "That's what you meant about catching 'a little of the flavor of Tolive.' Well, I caught more than a little, I caught a bellyful!"

Maddeningly patient, El sipped her drink, then said, "Just what did you see that so offended you?"

"I saw floggings!" Dalt sputtered. "Public floggings! The kind of thing that had been abandoned on Earth long before we ever left there!"

"Would you prefer *private* floggings?" There was a trace of a smile about her mouth.

"I would prefer no floggings, and I don't appreciate your sense of humor. I got a look at that woman's face and she was in pain."

"You see especially concerned over the fact that women as well as men were pilloried today."

"Maybe I'm just old-fashioned, but I don't like to see a woman beaten like that."

El eyed him over her glass. "There are a lot of old-fashioned things about you . . . do you know that you lapse into an archaic speech pattern when you get excited?" She shook herself abruptly. "But we'll go into that another time; right now I want to explore your high-handed attitude toward women.''

''Please—'' Dalt began, but she pushed on.

''I happen to be as mature, as responsible, as rational as any man I know, and if I commit a crime, I want you to assume that I knew exactly what I was doing. I'd take anything less as a personal insult.''

''Okay. Let's not get sidetracked on that age-old debate. The subject at hand is corporal punishment in a public place.''

''Was the flogging being done for sport?'' El asked. ''Were people standing around and cheering?''

''The answers are 'no' and 'no'—and don't start playing Socrates with me.''

El persisted. ''Did the lash slice deeply into their backs? Were they bleeding? Were they screaming with pain?''

''Stop the questions! No, they weren't screaming and they weren't bleeding, but they were most definitely in pain!''

''Why was this being done to these people?''

Dalt glared at her calm face for a long moment. ''Why are you doing this?''

''Because I have this feeling that you're going to be very important to IMC and I didn't want you to quietly slip away after you read the Contract.''

''The IMC contract? I read that and there's nothing—''

''Not that one. The Tolive Contract.''

''I don't understand,'' Dalt said with a quick shake of his head.

''I didn't think you would. I mean,'' she added quickly, ''that Dr. Webst was very excited about something this morning and I figured he never gave you your copy or explained anything about it.''

''Well, you're right on that account. I haven't the vaguest idea of what you're talking about.''

''Okay, then I'll take it upon myself to give you an outline of what you can expect from Tolive and what Tolive expects from you. The Contract sounds rather cold and terrible unless you know the background of the planet and understand the rationale for some of the clauses.''

''I don't think you should waste your breath.''

''Yes, you do. You're interested now, though you won't admit it.''

Dalt sighed reluctantly. ''I admit it. But I can't think of anything you can say that'll make public floggings look good.''

''Just listen.'' She finished her drink and signaled for another. ''Like most of the Federation member planets, Tolive was once a splinter world. It was settled by a very large group of anarchists who left Earth as one of the first splinter colonies. They bore no resemblance to the bearded, bomb-throwing stereotype from the old days of Earth, nor to the modern-day Broohnins. They merely held that no man has the right to rule another. A noble philosophy, wouldn't you say?''

Dalt gave a noncommittal shrug.

''Good. Like most anarchists of their day, however, they were anti-institutionalists. This eventually caused some major problems. They wanted no government at all: no police, no courts, no jails, no public works. Everything was to be handled by private firms. It took a couple of generations to set things up, and it worked quite well . . . at first. Then the private police forces got out of hand; they'd band together and take over a town and try to set up some sort of neofeudal state. Other police forces had to be hired to come in and roust them out, and there's be a lot of bloodshed and property destruction.'' She paused briefly as the waiter brought a fresh drink and El recommended that they order the vegetable platter.

''So,'' she continued, ''after this happened a few too many times, we—my ancestors, that is—decided that something had to be done to deal with the barbarians in our midst. After much debate, it was finally decided to create a bare minimum of public institutions: police, judiciary, penal, and administration.''

''No legislature?''

"No. They balked at creating posts for men who like to make rules to control other men; the very concept of a legislature was suspect—and still is, as far as I'm concerned. I mean, what kind of a man is it who wants to spend his life making plans and rules to alter or channel lives other than his own? There's a basic flaw in that kind of man."

"It's not so much a desire to rule," Dalt said. "With many it's merely a desire to be at the center of things, to be in on the big decisions."

"And those decisions mean power. They feel they are far better suited to make decisions about your life than you are. An ancient Earthman said it best: 'In every generation there are those who want to rule well—but they mean to rule. They promise to be good masters—but they mean to be masters.' His name was Daniel Webster."

"Never heard of him. But tell me: how can you have a judiciary if you have no law?"

"Oh, there's law—just no legislature. The minimum necessary legal code was formulated and incorporated into the Contract. Local police apprehend those who break the Contract and local judges determine to what extent it has been broken. The penal authority carries out the sentence, which is either public flogging or imprisonment."

"What?" Dalt said mockingly. "No public executions?"

El found no amusement in his attitude. "We don't kill people—someone just may be innocent."

"But you flog them! A person could die on that pillory!"

"That pillory is actually a highly sophisticated physiological monitor that measures physical pain in Gomler units. The judge decides how many Gomler units should be administered and the machine decides when that level has been reached relative to the individual in the pillory. If there are any signs of danger, the sentence is immediately terminated." They paused as the waiter placed the cold vegetable platters before them.

"He goes to prison then, I guess," Dalt said, eagerly biting into a mushroom-shaped tomato. Delicious.

"No. If he's undergone that much stress, he's considered a paid-up customer. Only our violent criminals go to jail."

Dalt looked bewildered. "Let me get this straight: Nonviolent criminals receive corporal punishment while violent criminals are merely locked away? That's a ridiculous paradox!"

"Not really. Is it better to take a young man such as the car thief out there today and lock him up with armed robbers, killers, and kidnapers? Why force a sneak thief to consort with barbarians and learn how to commit bigger and better crimes? We decided to break that old cycle. We prefer to put him through a little physical pain and a lot of public humiliation for a few minutes, and then let him go. His life is his own again, with no pieces missing. Our system is apparently working because our crime rate is incredibly low compared to other planets. Not out of fear, either, but because we've broken the crime-imprisonment-crime-imprisonment cycle. Recidivism is extremely low here!"

"But your violent criminals are merely sent to prison?"

"Right, but they're not allowed to consort with one another. The prison has historically acted as a nexus for the criminal subculture and so we decided to dodge that pitfall. We make no attempt at rehabilitation—that's the individual's job. The purpose of the prison on Tolive is to isolate the violent criminal from peaceful citizens and to punish him by temporarily or permanently depriving him of his freedom. He has a choice of either solitary confinement or of being blocked and put to work on a farm."

Dalt's eyes were wide. "A work farm! This sounds like the Dark Ages!"

"It's preferable to reconditioning him into a socially acceptable little robot, as is done on other, more 'enlightened' planets. We don't believe in tampering with a man's mind against his will; if he requests a mind block to make subjective time move more quickly, that's his decision.''

"But work farms!"

"They have to help earn their keep some way. A blocked prisoner has almost no volition; consequently, the farm overhead is low. He's put to work at simple agrarian tasks that are better done by machine, but this manages to defray some of the cost of housing and clothing him. When the block is finally removed—as is done once a year to give him the option of remaining blocked or returning to solitary—he is usually in better physical condition than when he started. However, there's a piece of his life missing and he knows it . . . and he doesn't soon forget. Of course, he may never request a block if he wishes to press his case before the court—but he spends his time in solitary, away from other criminals.''

"Seems awful harsh," Dalt muttered with a slow shake of his head.

El shrugged. "They're harsh men. They've used physical force or the threat of it to get what they want and we don't take kindly to that on Tolive. We insist that all relationships be devoid of physical coercion. We are totally free and therefore totally responsible for our actions—and we hold each other very close to that responsibility. It's in the Contract."

"But who is this Contract with?"

("It's 'whom,' ") Pard interjected.

Silence!

"Tolive," El replied.

"You mean the Tolivian government?"

"No, the planet itself. We declared our planet a person, just as corporations were declared legal entities many centuries ago."

"But why the planet?"

"For the sake of immutability. In brief: All humans of sound mind must sign the Contract within six months of their twentieth birthday—an arbitrary age; they can sign beforehand if they wish—or on their arrival on the planet. The Contract affirms the signer's right to pursue his own goals without interference from the government or other individuals. In return for a sum not to exceed more than five per cent of his annual income, this right will be protected by the agents of the planet—the police, courts, et cetera. But if the signer should inject physical coercion or the threat of it into any relationship, he must submit to the customary punishment, which we've already discussed. The Contract cannot be changed by future generations, thus we safeguard human rights from the tamperings of the fools, do-gooders, and powermongers who have destroyed every free society that has ever dared to rear its head along the course of human history.''

Dalt paused. "It all sounds so noble, yet you make a dangerous drug like Zemmelar freely available and you have stores that sell the most prurient, sick material I've ever seen."

"It's sold because there are people who want to buy it," El replied with another shrug. "If a signer wants to pollute his body with chemicals in order to visit an artificial Nirvana, that's his business. The drugs are available at competitive prices, so he doesn't have to steal to feed his habit; and he either learns how to handle his craving or he takes a cure, or he winds up dead from an overdose. And as for prurience, I suppose you stopped in at Lin's—he's our local pornographer. All I'll say about that is that I'm not for telling another individual how to enjoy himself . . . but didn't you hunt up any other lit shops? There's a big one on the square that sells nothing but classics: from *The Republic* to *No Treason* to *The Rigrod Chronicles*, from Aristotle to Hugo to Heinlein to Borjay. And down on BenTucker Drive is a shop specializing in new Tolivian works. But you never bothered to look for them."

"The scene in the park cut short my window shopping," Dalt replied tersely. They ate in silence for a moment and Pard took the opportunity to intrude.

("What're you thinking?")

I'm thinking that I don't know what to think.

("Well, in the meantime, ask her about that tax.")

Good idea! Dalt swallowed a mouthful and cleared his throat. "How do you justify a tax in a voluntary society?"

"It's in the Contract. A ceiling of five per cent was put on it because if a government spends much more than that, it's doing more than it should."

"But you don't even have any government to speak of; how does it spend even that much?"

"Federation dues, mostly: We have no army so we have to depend on the Fed Patrol for protection from external threat. The rest of the expenses go to the police, judiciary, and so on. We've never reached five per cent, by the way."

"So it's not a completely voluntary society, then," Dalt stated.

"Signing the Contract is voluntary, and that's what counts." She ran her napkin across her mouth. "And now I've got to run. Finish your meal and take your time and think about what we've discussed. If you want to stay, Webst will probably be waiting back at the complex. And don't worry about the bill . . . it's on me today." She leaned over, brushed her lips against his cheek, and was gone before Dalt could say a word.

("Quite an exit,") Pard said with admiration.

Quite a woman, Dalt replied, and went back to eating.

("Still ready to take the first shuttle out of here?")

I don't know. Everything seems to fit together in some weirdly logical way.

("Nothing weird about it at all. It works on the principle that humans will act responsibly if you hold them responsible for their actions. I find it rather interesting and want to spend some time here; and unless you want to start the fiercest argument of our partnership, you'll agree.")

Okay. We'll stay.

("No argument?")

None. I want to get to know El a little—a lot!—better.

("Glad to hear it.")

And the funny thing is: the more time I spend with

her, the less she reminds me of Jean.

("That's because she's really nothing at all like Jean; she's far more mature, far more intelligent. As a matter of fact, Ellen Lettre is one of the more fascinating things on this fascinating planet.")

Dalt's lack of response as he cleared his plate was tacit agreement. On the way out, his eye was caught by a golden seal on the door. It read: "Premises, kitchen, and food quality graded Class I by Nauch & Co., Inc." The date of the most recent inspection was posted below."

("I guess that's the Tolivian equivalent of a department of public health,") Pard said. ("Only this Nauch is probably a private company that works on a subscription basis. When you think about—")

Pard paused as a ground car whined to a halt before the restaurant and Dr. Webst leaped out. He looked relived at the sight of Dalt.

"Glad I found you," he said as he approached. "I met Dr. Lettre back at the complex and asked her when you were coming back; she said she wasn't sure if you were coming back at all."

"That was a possibility."

"Well, look, I don't know what this is all about, but you must come back to the complex with me immediately."

Dalt stiffened. "You're not trying to make an order out of that, I hope."

"No, of course not. It's just that I've made some startling discoveries about you that may have great medical significance. I've doubled-checked everything."

"What are you talking about?" Dalt had a sudden uneasy feeling.

Webst grabbed Dalt's arm and guided him toward the car. "I'm babbling, I know, but I'll explain everything on the way over to the complex." He paused in midstride. "Then again, maybe it's you who should do the explaining."

"Me?" Dalt was genuinely puzzled.

"Yes. Just who or what are you, Mr. Dalt?"

VIII

"THIS IS MY psi pattern," Webst said, pointing to an irregular red line undulating across the viewscreen in his office. "It shows the low level of activity found in the average human—nothing special about my psi abilities. Now, when we focus the detector on you, look what happens." He touched a panel and two green lines appeared on the screen. The one at the lower end was very similar to Webst's and occasionally superimposed itself on it at certain points.

"That's what I expected from you: another normal pattern. And I got it . . . but what the hell is that?" He was pointing to the large, smoothly flowing sine-wave configuration in the upper part of the screen. "We have tried this out on thousands of individuals and I have never once seen a pattern that even vaguely approximates that, neither in configuration nor in amplitude.

"Whatever it is," Webst continued as he blanked the screen, "it seems to like you, 'cause it goes where you go. At first I thought it was a malfunction, that's why I brought you over to Big Blue, where we have another model. But the same pattern appeared as soon as you walked into the building—and disappeared as soon as you left. So, what have you got to say for yourself, Mr. Dalt?"

Dalt shrugged with convincing bafflement. "I really

don't know what to say." Which was true. His mind
raced in an attempt to give Webst, obviously an expert
in psionics, a plausible but fictitious explanation. The
machine in question was a fairly recent development of
IMC research—it detected levels of psionic capacity,
even in the nascent stage, and was planned for interplanetary marketing to the psi schools which were
springing up on every planet. The current thrust of
Webst's research was in the field of psionics and
psychotherapy, so he took the liberty of screening for
psi ability everyone who entered his office. He felt he
had hit pay dirt with Dalt.

"You mean to say that you've never had any inkling
of psi ability?" Webst asked. Dalt shook his head.
"Well then, are there any blank spots in your memory
. . . do you ever find yourself somewhere and can't recall how you got there?"

"What are you driving at?"

"I'm looking for a dissociative reaction or a second
personality—something, anything, to explain that second level of activity. I don't want to alarm you," he
said gently, "but you're only allowed one: one mind,
one psi level. The only conclusion I can draw is that you
either have two minds or the most unusual single mind
in the galaxy."

("He was right the first time.")

I know, but what do we do?

("Play dumb, of course. We wanted to get out of
microbiology and into psych—this may be our
chance.")

Dalt mulled this over. Finally, "This is all very interesting, Dr. Webst, but quite meaningless as far as my
professional life is concerned." *That should put the
conversation on the track we want.*

"That's what I'd like to discuss with you," Webst replied. "If I can get a release from Dr. Hyne, would you
be interested in spending some time with my department
assisting us with some experiments?"

"Just what kind of experiments?"

Webst came around his desk to stand before Dalt.

"I've been trying to find a use for psionics in psychotherapy. We are daily trying to probe the minds of these so-called horrors cases in an effort to find out why they don't respond to conventional therapy. I have no doubt that it's the path of the future—all we need is the right technology and the right psi talents.

"Remember Sally Ragna? The girl who hides in the corner and no known psychotherapy can reach? That's the kind of patient I'm after. We've developed an instrument to magnify psi powers, and right now a man with one per cent of your aptitude is trying to get a look inside her mind." Webst suddenly stiffened and his eyes burned into Dalt. "Right now! Would you come over to Big Blue right now and give it a try? All I want you to do is take a quick look—just go in and out, no more!"

("This is our chance,") Pard urged. ("Take it!") He was obviously anxious to give it a try.

"All right," said Dalt, who had a few reservations lurking in the back of his mind. "Might as well give it a try and see if anything at all can be done."

In Big Blue they seated him before Sally Ragna, who wasn't cringing now, due to heavy sedation. The psi booster Webst had mentioned, a gleaming silver disk, was slung above them.

This is a waste of time, Dalt told Pard.

("I don't think so. I've learned one thing, anyway: That machine of Webst's isn't worth a damn—I'm not getting a bit of boost from it. But I don't think I'll need it. I've made a few probes using the same technique I played with on the liner and I'm meeting with very little resistance. I'm sure I can get in. One thing, though . . . I'm going to have to take you with me.")

I don't know if I like that.

("It's necessary, I'm afraid. I'll need every ounce of reserve function to stay oriented once I get in there, and I may even have to draw on your meager psi power.")

Dalt hesitated. The thought of confronting madness on its own ground was deeply frightening. His stomach lurched as he replied, *Okay, let's do it. But be careful!*

("I'm frightened too, friend.")

The thought flashed across Dalt's mind that he had never before considered the possibility of Pard being frightened of anything. Concerned, yes . . . but frightened—

The thought disappeared as his view of Sally Ragna and the room around them swirled away and he entered the place where Sally was spending her life:

/countless scintillating pinpoints of light that somehow gave off no illumination poured into treelike shapes/a sky of violet shot thorugh with crimson flashes that throw shadows in paradoxical directions/an overall dimness that half obscures living fungus forms that crawl and leap and hang from the pointillistic trees/

/moving forward now/

/past a cube of water with schools of fish each made of two opposing tails swimming forever in stasis/ mountains crumble to the right/breach-born ahead is a similar range/which disappears as they step off a sudden precipice and float through a dank forest and are surrounded by peering, glowing, unblinking yellow eyes/

/descent/

/to a desert road stretching emptily and limitlessly ahead/and suddenly a town has sprung up around them, its buildings built at impossible angles/a stick man walks up and smiles as his form fills out and then swells, bloats, and ruptures, spewing mounds of writhing maggots upon the ground/the face and body begin to dissolve but the mouth remains, growing larger and nearer/it opens to show its double rows of curved teeth/ and growing still larger it moves upon them, enveloping them, closing upon them with a SNAP/

Dalt next found himself on the floor with Webst and a technician bending over him. But it was Pard who awakened him.

("Get up, Steve! Now! We've got to go back in there as soon as possible!")

Dalt rose slowly to his feet and brushed his palms. "I'm all right," he told Webst. "Just slipped out of the chair." And to Pard: *You must be kidding!*

("I assure you, I am not. That was a jolting experience, and if we don't go back immediately, we'll probably build up a reflex resistance that will keep us out in the future.")

That's fine with me.

("But we can do something for this girl; I'm sure of it.")

Dalt waved Webst and his technician away. "I'm going to try again," he muttered, and repositioned himself before the girl. *Okay, Pard. I'm trusting you.*

/and then they were in a green-fogged bog as ochre hands reached up for them from the rank marsh grasses to try to pull them into the quicksand/

/the sun suddenly appeared overhead but was quickly muffled by the fog/it persisted, however, and slowly the fog began to thin and burn away/

/the land tilted then and the marsh began to drain/the rank grasses began to wither and die in the sun/slowly a green carpet of neatly trimmed grass unrolled about them, covering and smothering the ever-clutching hands/

/a giant, spheroid boulder rolled in from the horizon at dazzling speed and threatened to overrun them until a chasm yawned suddenly before it and swallowed it/

/dark things crept toward them from all sides, trailing dusk behind them, but a high, smooth, safe wall suddenly encircled them and sunlight prevailed/

Dalt was suddenly back in the room again with Sally Ragna, only this time he was seated on the chair instead of the floor.

("We'll leave her in that sanctuary by herself for a few minutes while I get the lay of the land here.")

You made all those changes, then?

("Yes, and it was easier than I thought it would be. I met a lot of resistance at first when I tried to bring the sun out, but once I accomplished that, I seemed to be in full control. There were a couple of attempts to get at her again, but they were easily repulsed.")

What now?

("Now that we've made her comfortable in her sylvan

nunnery—which is as unreal as the horror show she's lived in all these years, but completely unthreatening—we'll bring her back to reality.'')

Ah, but what is reality?

("Please, Steve. I haven't time for such a sophomoric question. Just go along with me, and for a working definition we'll just say that reality is what trips you up when you walk around with your eyes closed. But no more talk . . . now comes the hard part. Up until now we've been seeing what she sees; the task at hand is to reverse that situation. Here goes.'')

They were back in again and apparently Pard's benign reconstruction had held—and had been improved upon; the wall had been removed and a smooth grassy sward stretched to the far horizon. Pard set up a bare green panel to the left; three more panels appeared and boxed them in . . . a lighted ceiling finished the job. An odd piece of metallic machinery overhung them, and there, just a short distance before them, sat a man with a golden hand and a flamestone slung at his throat, whose dark hair was interrupted by a patch of silver at the crown.

A sudden blurring and they were looking at Sally again. Only this time she was looking back—and smiling. As tears slid down her cheeks, the smile faded and she collapsed into unconsciousness.

IX

"YOU'VE DONE SOMETHING," Webst said later at the office after Sally had been examined and returned to her bed, "something beneficial. Can't be sure just yet, but I can smell it! Did you see her smile at you? She's never smiled before. Never!"

Webst's enthusiasm whirled past Dalt without the slightest effect. He was tired, tired as he'd never been before. There was a vague feeling of dissociation, too; he'd visited the mind of another and had returned home to find himself subtly altered by the experience.

"Well, I certainly hope I didn't go through all that for nothing."

"I'm sure you didn't," said a voice behind him. He turned to see El walking across the room. "She's sleeping now," she said, sliding easily into a chair, "and without a hypnotic. You've gotten through to her, no question about it."

Webst leaned forward on his desk. "But just what is it you've done?" he asked intently. "What did you see in there?"

Dalt opened his mouth to protest, to put off all explanations and descriptions until tomorrow, but Pard cut him off.

("Tell them something. They're hungry for information.")

How can I describe all . . . that?

("Try. Just skim the details.")

Dalt gave a halting summary of what they had seen and done, then:

"In conclusion, it's my contention that the girl's underlying lesion was not organic but conceptual. Her sense of reality was completely aberrant, but as to how this came to be, I do not know." He hesitated and El thought she saw him shudder ever so slightly. "For a moment I got the feeling that I was working against something . . . something dark and very alien, just over the horizon. At one point I thought I actually touched it, or it reached for me, or—" He shook himself. "I don't know. Maybe it was part of her fantasy complex. Anyway, what matters is that she was a very sick girl and I think I've helped her."

"I take it, then," Webst said, "that we can assume that these acute, unremitting, chemonegative schizophrenics are actually only conceptually deranged. Okay, I'll buy that. But *why* are they deranged?"

Dalt remembered the dark thing he had sensed in Sally's mind and the word "imposed" rushed into his thoughts, but he pushed it away. "Can't help you there as yet. But let's get her back on her feet and worry about why it happened later on. Chemotherapy was no good because her enzyme chains are normal; and psychotherapy has been useless because, as far as this patient was concerned, the psychotherapist didn't exist. Apparently, only a strong psionic thrust and subsequent reconstruction of the fantasy world is of any value. And by the way, her mind was extremely easy to enter. Perhaps in erecting an impenetrable barrier against reality, it left itself completely open to psionics."

El and Webst were virtually glowing with the exhilaration of discovery. "This is incredible!" Webst declared. "A whole new direction in psychotherapy! Mr. Dalt, I don't know how we can repay you!"

("Tell him what he can pay you.")

We can't take money for helping that poor girl!

("He's going to ask you to do it again . . . and again.

That was no sylvan picnic in there—it's risky business. I won't allow us to enter another mind unless we're compensated for it. Value given for value received, remember?'')

That's crass.

("That's life. Something that costs nothing is usually worth the price.")

That's trite.

("But true. Quote him a figure.")

Dalt thought for a moment, then said, "I'll require a fee for Sally . . . and any others you want me to try." He named a sum.

"That sounds reasonable." Webst nodded. "I won't dicker with you."

El's face reflected amusement tinged with amazement. "You're full of surprises, aren't you?"

Webst smiled too. "He's welcome to every credit we can spare if he can bring those horrors patients around. We'll even try to get a bigger budget. I'll talk to Dr. Hyne and have you transferred to this department; meanwhile, there's an ethical question you should consider. You are in effect performing an experimental procedure on mentally incompetent patients who are incapable of giving their consent."

"What about their guardians?"

"These patients have no guardians, no identity. And a guardian would be irrelevant as far as the ethical question is concerned—that is up to you. In the physician role, you've got to decide whether an experimental procedure—or even an established procedure—will have a greater chance of benefiting the patient than doing harm to him, and whether the possible benefits are worth the risk. And the patient must come first; not humanity, not science, but the *patient*. Only you can decide."

"I made that decision before I invaded Sally," Dalt replied with a touch of acid. "The gains were mutual: I would learn something, she would, hopefully, receive therapeutic value. The risks, as far as I could foresee, would all be mine."

Webst considered this. "Mr. Dalt," he said finally,

"I think you and I are going to get along just fine." He extended his hand and Dalt grasped it firmly.

El came to his side and hooked her arm around his. "Welcome to the department," she said with a half smile tugging at the corners of her mouth. "This is quite a turnaround from the man who swore a few hours ago that he was taking the next shuttle out."

"I haven't forgotten that episode, believe me. I can't quite accept the code you Tolivians live by as yet, but I think I'd like to stick around and see if it works as well as you say it does."

The viewphone had beeped again while they were talking. Webst took the call, then suddenly headed for the door. "That was Big Blue—Sally just woke up and asked for a drink of water!" Nothing more needed to be said; El and Dalt immediately fell in behind him as he made his way to the carport.

The last sanguine rays of the sun slipping into the plaza found the ambulatory patients clustered in hushed, muttering knots. And all eyes suddenly became riveted on the car that held Webst, Dalt, and El as it pulled up beside Big Blue. An elderly woman broke away from a small group and came forward, squinting at the trio in the waning light.

"It's him!" she cried hoarsely as she reached the car. "He's got the silver patch of hair, the flamestone, and the golden hand that heals!" She clutched the back of Dalt's suit as he turned away. "Touch me with your healing hand!" she cried. "My mind is sick and only you can help me! Please! I'm not as sick as Sally was!"

"No, wait!" Dalt said, whirling and shrinking away. "It doesn't work that way!"

But the woman seemed not to hear him, repeating, "Heal me! Heal me!" And over her shoulder he could see the other patients in the plaza crowding forward.

Webst was suddenly at his side, his face close, his eyes shining in the fading darkness. "Go ahead," he whispered excitedly, "touch her. You don't have to do anything else, just reach out that left hand and lay it on her head."

Dalt hesitated; then, feeling foolish, pressed the heel of his palm against her forehead. The woman covered her face at his touch and scurried away, muttering, "Thank you, thank you," through her hands.

With that, it was as if a dam had burst. The patients were suddenly swirling all around him and Dalt found himself engulfed by a torrent of outstretched hands and cries of, "Heal me! Heal me! Heal me! Heal me!" He was pushed, pulled, his clothes and limbs were plucked at, and it was only with great difficulty that El and Webst managed to squeeze him through the press of supplicants and into the quiet of Big Blue.

"Now you know why he's at the top of his profession," El said softly, nodding her head toward Webst as she pressed a drink into Dalt's hand, a hand that even now, in the security of Big Blue, betrayed a slight but unmistakable tremor. The experience in the plaza had unnerved him—the hands, the voices, reaching and crying for him in the twilight, seeking relief from the psychological and physiological afflictions burdening them; the incident, though only moments past, was becoming increasingly surreal in retrospect.

He shook himself and took a deep gulp of the drink. "I don't follow."

"The way he sized up the situation immediately as mass hysteria and put it to good use: the enormity of placebo effect in medicine has never been fully appreciated, even to this day. There were a lot of chronically ill patients in that plaza who had heard of a man who performed a miraculous cure and they all wanted a piece of that miracle for themselves."

"But how did they find out?"

El laughed. "The grapevine through these wards could challenge a subspace laser for speed of transmission!"

Webst flicked off the viewphone from which he had been receiving a number of hurried reports, and turned to them, grinning. "Well, the blind see, the deaf hear, and the lame walk," he announced, then burst out laughing at the horrified expression on Dalt's face.

"No, nothing as dramatic as that, I'm afraid, but we have had a few remarkable symptomatic remissions."

"Not because of me!" Dalt snapped, his tone betraying annoyance. "I didn't do a thing—those people only think I did."

"*Exactly!* You didn't cure them per se, but you did act as a catalyst through which the minds of those people could gain some leverage on their bodies."

"So I'm a faith-healer, in other words."

"Out in the plaza, you were—and still are, now more than ever. We have a rare opportunity here to study the phenomenon of the psychosomatic cure, something which fascinates the student of behavior more than anything else. It's the power of the mind over the body in action . . . we know almost nothing of the dynamics of the relationship."

("I could tell them a few things about that,") Pard muttered.

You've said quite enough tonight, friend.

"And you're a perfect focal point," Webst added. "You have a genuine healing ability in a certain area, and this along with an undeniably unique appearance evidently works to give you an almost messianic aura in susceptible minds."

("Defensively worded in the best scientific tradition.")

Webst continued in lowered tones, talking to himself more than to anyone else. "You know, I don't see why the same phenomenon couldn't be duplicated on any other planet in the human system, and on a much larger scale. Every planet has its share of horrors cases and they're all looking for a way to handle them. If we limit the amount of information we release—such as keeping your identity a secret—the inevitable magnification that occurs with word-of-mouth transmission will have you raising the dead by the time you finish your work here. And by then every human planet will be clamoring for your services. And while you're reconstructing sick minds, Dr. Lettre and I will be carefully observing the epiphenomena."

"Meaning the psychosomatic cures?"

El nodded, getting caught up in Webst's vision. "Right. And it would be good for Tolive, too. He-Who-Heals-Minds—pardon the dramatic phrasing—will come from Tolive, and that should counteract some of the smears being spread around."

"How does that sound, Mr. Dalt . . . or should I say, 'Healer'?"

What do you think?

("Sounds absolutely wonderful to me, as long as we don't start to believe what people will be saying about us.")

"Interesting," Dalt replied slowly, "very interesting. But why don't we see how things go here on Tolive before we start star-hopping." He had a lot of adjustments to make, physically and intellectually, if he was going to spend any time here.

"Right!" Webst said, and headed back to the viewphone. "And I'm sure it's been a long day for you. I'll have the plaza cleared and you can return to your hotel as soon as you like."

"That's not the place I had in mind," Dalt muttered to El, "but I guess the sunset's long gone by now out there on the plain."

El shrugged warmly. "The sunrise is just as good."

INTERLUDE:

A Soliloquy for Two

Can't you do anything?

("I've already tried . . . a number of times. And failed.")

I didn't know that. Why didn't you tell me?

("I know how much she means to you, so I made the attempts on my own. The most recent was yesterday. When you entered her body, I entered her mind—that seems to be her most vulnerable moment.")

And?

("The cells won't respond. I'm unable to exert any influence over the components of another body. They simply will not respond.")

Oh.

A long pause, then an audible sigh.

All things must pass, eh?

("Except us.")

Yeah. Except us.

YEAR 271

The Healer's advent coincided with a period of political turmoil within the Federation. The Restructurist movement was agitating with steadily increasing influence for a more active role by the Federation in planetary and interplanetary affairs. This attitude directly contradicted the laissez-faire orientation of the organization's charter.

His departure from human affairs occurred as political friction was reaching its peak and was as abrupt as his arrival. Certain scholars claim that he was killed in a liner crash off Tarvodet, and there is some evidence to support this.

His more fanatical followers, however, insist that he is immortal and was driven from his calling by political forces. Their former premise is obviously ridiculous, but the latter may well have some basis in fact.

from *The Healer: Man & Myth*

by Emmerz Fent

X

THE HEALER, the most recognizable figure in the human galaxy, stood gloved, cloaked, cowled, and unrecognized amid the small group of mourners as the woman's body was tenderly placed within the machine that would reduce it to its component elements. He felt no need for tears. She had lived her life to the fullest, the latter half of it at his side. And when the youth treatments had finally become ineffective and she'd begun to notice a certain blurring on the perimeters of her intellectual function, she ended her life, calmly and quietly, to insure that she'd be remembered by her lover as the proud woman she had always been, not the lesser person she might become. And only The Healer, her lover, knew how she had died.

The wrinkled little man next to him suspected, of course. And approved. They and the others watched in silence as the machine swallowed her body, and all drank deeply of the air about them as it became filled with her molecules, each witness trying to incorporate into himself a tiny part of a cherished friend.

The old man looked at his companion, who had never deigned to show a year's worth of aging in all the time he had known him—at least not on the surface. But there had been strain and fatigue growing behind the eyes during the past few years. A half century of sickness and deformity of mind and body, outstretched hands and blank eyes lay behind him and possibly endless years of the same awaited him.

"You look weary, my friend."

"I am." The others began to drift away. "It all seems so futile. For every mind I open, two more are reported newly closed. The pressure continually mounts—'come to us'—'no, come to us, we need you more!' Everywhere I go I'm preceded by arguments, threats, and bribes between vying clinics and planets. I seem to have become a commodity."

The old man nodded with understanding. "Where to now?"

"Into private practice of some sort, I suppose. I've stayed with IMC this long only because of you . . . and her. As a matter of fact, a certain sector representative is waiting for me now. DeBloise is the name."

"A Restructurist. Be careful."

"I will." The Healer smiled. "But I'll hear what he has to say. Stay well, friend," he said and walked away.

The wrinkled man gazed wistfully after him. "Ah, if only I had your talent for that."

Sector Representative DeBloise had for some time considered himself quite an important man, yet it took him a few minutes to adjust to the presence of the individual seated calmly across the desk from him, a man of unmistakable appearance who had gained almost mythical stature in the past few decades: The Healer.

"In brief, sir," DeBloise said with the very best of his public smiles, "we of the Restructurist movement wish to encourage you to come to our worlds. You seem to have made a habit of avoiding us in the past."

"That's because I worked through the IMC network in which the Restructurist worlds refuse to participate . . . something to do with the corps' support of the LaNague charter, I'm told."

"That's part of it." The smile became more ingratiating as he said, "Politics seems to work its way into everything, doesn't it. But that's irrelevant now, since it was the news that you'd no longer be with IMC that brought me here to Tolive. I want you to come to Jebinose; our Bureau of Medicine and Research will pay all your fees."

"I'm sorry," the Healer said slowly, "but I deal only with patients, not with governments."

"Well, if you mean to come to Jebinose and practice independently of the Bureau, I'm afraid we couldn't allow that. You see, we've set very high and very rigid standards for the practice of medicine on our planet and I'm afraid allowing you such license, despite your reputation, would set a bad precedent."

"If a patient wishes my services, he or his guardian should be free to engage them. Why should some bureau have anything to say in the matter?"

"What you ask is impossible," DeBloise said with a shake of his head. "Our people must be protected from being duped by frauds."

The Healer's smile was rueful as he rose to his feet. "That is quite evident. And thus Jebinose is not for me."

DeBloise's face suddenly hardened, the smile forgotten. "It's quite evident to me, *Healer*"—he spat the word—"that you've spent too much time among these barbaric Tolivians. All right, play your game: but I think you should know that a change is in the wind and that we shall soon be running the entire Federation *our* way. And when we do, we'll see to it that every planet gets its fair share of your services!"

"Perhaps there will be no Healer, then," came the quiet reply.

"Don't try to bluff me!" DeBloise laughed. "I know your type. You glory in the adulation that greets you everywhere you go. It's more addicting than Zemmelar." There was a trace of envy in his voice. "But Restructurists are not so easily awed. You are a man—a uniquely talented one, yes, but still just one man—and when the tide turns for us, you will join in the current or be swept under."

The Healer's eyes blazed but his voice was calm.

"Thank you, Mr. DeBloise. You have just clarified a problem and prompted a decision that has been growing increasingly troublesome over the past decade or so." He turned and strode from the room.

Nearly two and a half centuries passed before The Healer was seen again.

YEAR 505

Not long after the disappearance of The Healer, the so-called DeBloise scandal came to the fore. The subsequent Restructurist walk-out led to the Federation-Restructurist civil war ("war" is hardly a fitting term for those sporadic skirmishes) which was eventually transformed into a full-scale interracial war when the Tarks decided to interfere. It was during the height of the Terro-Tarkan conflict that the immortality myth of The Healer was born.

Oblivious to the wars, the horrors continued to appear at a steady rate and the psychosciences had gained little ground against the malady. For that reason, perhaps, a man with a stunning resemblance to The Healer appeared and began to cure the horrors with an efficacy that rivaled that of the original. Thus an historical figure became a legend.

Who he was and why he chose to appear at that particular moment remains a mystery.

from *The Healer: Man & Myth*

by Emmerz Fent

XI

DALT LOCKED THE flitter into the roof cradle, released the controls, and slumped into the seat.

("There. Don't you feel better now?") Pard asked.

"No," Dalt replied aloud. "I feel tired. I just want to go to bed."

("You'll thank me in the morning. Your mental outlook will be better, and you won't even be stiff because I've been putting you through isometrics in your sleep every night.")

"No wonder I wake up tired in the morning!"

("Mental fatigue, Steve. *Mental*. We've both gotten too involved in this project and the strain is starting to tell.")

"Thanks a lot," he muttered as he slid from the cab and shuffled to the door. "The centuries have not dulled your talent for stating the obvious."

And it was obvious. After The Healer episode, Dalt and Pard had shifted interests from the life sciences to the physical sciences and pursued their studies amid the Federation-Restructurist war without ever noticing it. That muddled conflict had been about ready to die out after a century or so, due to lack of interest, when a new force injected itself into the picture. The Tarks, in an attempt at subterfuge as clumsy as their previous attempts at diplomacy, declared a unilateral alliance with the

Restructurist coalition and promptly attacked a number
of Federation bases along a disputed stretch of expansion border. Divide and conquer is a time-tested ploy,
but the Tarks neglected to consider the racial variable.
Humans have little compunction about killing each
other over real or imagined differences, but there is an
archetypical repugnance at the thought of an alien race
taking such a liberty. And so the Feds and Restructurists
promptly united and declared *jihad* on the Tarkan Empire.

Naturally, weapons research blossomed and physi-
cists became very popular. Dalt's papers on field theory
engendered numerous research offers from companies
anxious to enter the weapons market. The Tarkan force
shield was allowing their ships to penetrate deep into
Terran territory with few losses, and thus became a
prime target for big companies like Star Ways, whose
offer Dalt accepted.

The grind of high-pressure research, however, was
beginning to take its toll on Dalt; and Pard, ever the
physiopsychological watchdog, had finally prevailed in
convincing Dalt to shorten his workday and spend a few
hours on the exercise courts.

Wearily, Dalt tapped out the proper code on the entry
plate and the door slid open. Even now, drained as he
was in body and mind, he realized that his thoughts
were starting to drift toward the field-negation problem
at Star Ways labs. He was about to try to shift his train
of thought when a baritone voice did it for him.

"Do you often talk to yourself, Mr. Cheserak? Or
should I call you Mr. Dalt? Or would you prefer Mr.
Storgen?" The voice came from a dark, muscular man
who had made himself comfortable in one of the living-
room chairs; he was pointing a blaster at the center of
Dalt's chest. "Or how about Mr. Quet?" he continued
with a self-assured smile, and Dalt noticed two other
men, partly in shadow, standing behind him. "Come
now! Don't just stand there. Come in and sit down.
After all, this *is* your home."

Eyeing the weapon that followed his every move, Dalt

chose a chair opposite the intruders. "What do you want?"

"Why, your secret, of course. We thought you'd be out longer and had hardly begun our search of the premises when we heard your flitter hit the dock. Very rude of you to interrupt us."

Dalt shook his head grimly at the thought of humans conspiring against their own race. "Tell your Tark friends that we're no closer to piercing their force shields than we were when the war started."

The dark man laughed with genuine amusement. "No, my friend, I assure you that our sympathies concerning the Terro-Tarkan war are totally orthodox. Your work at Star Ways is of no interest to us."

"Then what do you want?" he repeated, his eyes darting to the other two figures, one a huge, steadfast hulk, the other slight and fidgety. All three, like Dalt, wore the baggy coversuits with matching peaked skullcaps currently in fashion in this end of the human part of the galaxy. "I keep my money in a bank, so—"

"Yes, I know," the seated man interrupted. "I know which bank and I know exactly how much. And I also have a list of all the other accounts you have spread among the planets of this sector."

"How in the name of—"

The stranger held up his free hand and smiled. "None of us has been properly introduced. What shall we call you, sir? Which of your many aliases do you prefer?"

Dalt hesitated, then said, "Dalt," grudgingly.

"Excellent! Now, Mr. Dalt, allow me to introduce Mr. Hinter"—indicating the hulk—"and Mr. Giff" —the fidget. "I am Aaron Kanlos and up until two standard years ago I was a mere president of an Interstellar Brotherhood of Computer Technicians local on Ragna. Then one of our troubleshooters working for the Tellalung Banking Combine came to me with an interestingly anomaly and my life changed. I became a man with a mission: to find you."

As Dalt sat in silence, denying Kanlos the satisfaction of being told to go on, Pard said, ("I don't like the way he said that.'')

"I was told," Kanlos finally went on, "that a man named Marten Quet had deposited a check from Interstellar Business Advisers in an account he had just opened. The IBA check cleared but the man didn't." Again he looked to Dalt for a reaction. Finding a blank stare, he continued:

"The computer, it seems, was insisting that this Mr. Quet was really a certain Mr. Galdemar and duly filed an anomaly slip which one of our technicians picked up. These matters are routine on a planet such as Ragna, which is a center for intrigue in the interstellar business community; keeping a number of accounts under different names is the rule rather than the exception in those circles. So, the usual override code was fed in, but the machine still would not accept the anomaly. After running a negative check for malfunction, the technician ordered a full printout on the two accounts." Kanlos smiled at this. "That's illegal, of course, but his curiosity was piqued. The pique became astonishment when he read the listings, and so naturally he brought the problem to his superior."

("I'm sure he did!") Pard interjected, ("Some of these computer-union bosses have a tidy little blackmail business on the side.")

Be quiet! Dalt hissed mentally.

"There were amazing similarities," Kanlos was saying. "Even in the handwriting, although one was right-handed and the other obviously left-handed. Secondly, their fingerprints were very much alike, one being merely a distortion of the other. Both were very crude methods of deception. Nothing unusual there. The retinal prints were, of course, identical; that was why the computer had filed an anomaly. So why was the technician so excited? And why had the computer ignored the override code? As I said, multiple accounts are hardly unusual." Kanlos paused for dramatic effect, then: "The answer was to be found in the opening dates of the accounts. Mr. Quet's account was only a few days old . . . Mr. Galdemar's had been opened two hundred years ago!

"I was skeptical at first, at least until I did some research on retinal prints and found that two identical sets cannot exist. Even clones have variations in the vessels of the eyegrounds. So, I was faced with two possibilities: either two men generations apart possessed identical retinal patterns, or one man has been alive much longer than any man should be. The former would be a mere scientific curiosity; the latter would be of monumental importance."

Dalt shrugged. "The former possibility is certainly more likely than the latter."

"Playing coy, eh?" Kanlos smiled. "Well, let me finish my tale so you'll fully appreciate the efforts that brought me to your home. Oh, it wasn't easy, my friend, but I knew there was a man roaming this galaxy who was well over two hundred years old and I was determined to find him. I sent out copies of the Quet/Galdemar retinal prints to all the other locals in our union, asking them to see if they could find accounts with matching patterns. It took time, but then the reports began to trickle back—different accounts on different planets with different names and fingerprints, but always the same retinal pattern. There was also a huge trust fund—a truly staggering amount of credits —on the planet Myrna in the name of Cilo Storgen, who also happens to have the Quet/Galdemar pattern.

"You may be interested to know that the earliest record found was that of a man known simply as 'Dalt,' who had funds transferred from an account on Tolive to a bank on Neeka about two and a quarter centuries ago. Unfortunately, we have no local on Tolive, so we couldn't backtrack from there. The most recent record was, of course, the one on Ragna belonging to Mr. Galdemar. He left the planet and disappeared, it seems. However, shortly after his disappearance, a Mr. Cheserak—who had the same retinal prints as Mr. Galdemar and all of the others, I might add—opened an account here on Meltrin. According to the bank, Mr. Cheserak lives here . . . alone." Kanlos's smile took on a malicious twist. "Care to comment on this, Mr. Dalt?"

Dalt was outwardly silent but an internal dispute was rapidly coming to a boil.

Congratulations, mastermind!

("Don't go putting the blame on me!") Pard countered. ("If you'll just think back, you'll remember that I told you—")

You told me—guaranteed me, in fact—that nobody'd ever connect all those accounts. As it turns out, you might as well have left a trail of interstellar beacons!

("Well, I just didn't think it was necessary to go to the trouble of changing our retinal print. Not that it would have been difficult—neovascularization of the retina is no problem—but I thought changing names and fingerprints would be enough. Multiple accounts are necessary due to shifting economic situations, and I contend that no one would have caught on if you hadn't insisted on opening that account on Ragna. I warned you that we already had an account there, but you ignored me.")

Dalt gave a mental snort. *I ignored you only because you're usually so overcautious. I was under the mistaken impression that you could handle a simple little deception, but—*

The sound of Kanlos's voice brought the argument to a halt. "I'm waiting for a reply, Mr. Dalt. My research shows that you've been around for two and a half centuries. Any comment?"

"Yes." Dalt sighed. "Your research is inaccurate."

"Oh, really?" Kanlos's eyebrows lifted. "Please point out my error, if you can."

Dalt spat out the words with reluctant regret. "I'm twice that age."

Kanlos half started out of his chair. "Then it's true!" His voice was hoarse. "Five centuries . . . incredible!"

Dalt shrugged with annoyance. "So what?"

"What do you mean, 'so what?' You've found the secret of immortality, trite as that phrase may be, and I've found you. You appear to be about thirty-five years old, so I assume that's when you began using whatever it is you use. I'm forty now and don't intend to get any older. Am I getting through to you, Mr. Dalt?"

Dalt nodded. "Loud and clear." To Pard: *Okay, what do I tell him?*

("How about the truth? That'll be just about as useful to him as any fantastic tale we can concoct on the spur of the moment.")

Good idea. Dalt cleared his throat. "If one wishes to become immortal, Mr. Kanlos, one need only take a trip to the planet Kwashi and enter a cave there. Before long, a sluglike creature will drop off the cave ceiling onto your head; cells from the slug will invade your brain and set up an autonomous symbiotic mind with consciousness down to the cellular level. In its own self-interest, this mind will keep you from aging or even getting sick. There is a slight drawback, however: Legend on the planet Kwashi has it that only one in a thousand will survive the ordeal. I happen to be one who did."

"I don't consider this a joking matter," Kanlos said with an angry frown.

"Neither do I!" Dalt replied, his eyes cold as he rose to his feet. "Now I think I've wasted just about enough time with this charade. Put your blaster away and get out of my house! I keep no money here and no elixirs of immortality or whatever it is you hope to find. So take your two—"

"*That will be enough, Mr. Dalt!*" Kanlos shouted. He gestured to Hinter. "Put the cuff on him!"

The big man lumbered forward carrying a sack in his right hand. From it he withdrew a metal globe with a shiny cobalt surface that was interrupted only by an oval aperture. Dalt's hands were inserted there as Giff came forward with a key. The aperture tightened around Dalt's wrists as the key was turned and the sphere suddenly became stationary in space. Dalt tried to pull it toward him but it wouldn't budge, nor could he push it away. It moved freely, however, along a vertical axis.

("A gravity cuff,") Pard remarked. ("I've read about them but never expected to be locked into one.")

What does it do?

("Keeps you in one spot. It's favored by many law-enforcement agencies. When activated, it locks onto an axis through the planet's center of gravity. Motion along that axis is unrestricted, but that's it; you can't go anywhere else. This seems to be an old unit. The newer ones are supposedly much smaller.")

In other words, we're stuck.

("Right.")

". . . and so that ought to keep you safe and sound while we search the premises," Kanlos was saying, his veneer of civility restored. "But just to make sure that nothing happens to you," he smiled, "Mr. Giff will stay with you."

"You won't find anything," Dalt said doggedly, "because there isn't anything to find."

Kanlos eyed him shrewdly. "Oh, we'll find something all right. And don't think I was taken in by your claim of being five hundred years old. You're two hundred fifty and that's about it—but that's longer than any man should live. I traced you back to Tolive, which happens to be the main research center of the Interstellar Medical Corps. I don't think it's a coincidence that the trail ends there. Something was done to you there and I intend to find out what."

"I tell you, nothing was—"

Kanlos held up a hand. "Enough! The matter is too important to bandy words about. I've spent two years and a lot of money looking for you and I intend to make that investment pay off. Your secret is worth untold wealth and hundreds of years of life to the man who controls it. If we find no evidence of what we're looking for on the premises, we'll come back to you, Mr. Dalt. I deplore physical violence and shall refrain from using it until I have no other choice. Mr. Hinter here does not share my repugnance for violence. If our search of the lower levels is fruitless, *he* will deal with you." So saying, he turned and led Hinter below.

Giff watched them go, then strode quickly to Dalt's side. He made a hurried check of the gravcuff, seemed satisfied, then stole off to one of the darker corners of the room. Seating himself on the floor, he reached into his pocket and removed a silvery disk; with his left hand he pushed back his skullcap and parted the hair atop his head. The disk was attached here as Giff leaned back against the wall and closed his eyes. Soon, a vague smile began to play around his lips.

("A button-head!") Pard exclaimed.

Looks that way. This is a real high-class crew we're mixed up with. Look at him! Must be one of those sexual recordings.

Giff had begun to writhe on the floor, his legs twisting, flexing, and extending with pleasure.

("I'm surprised you don't blame yourself for it.")

I do, in a way—

("Knew it!")

—even if it is a perversion of the circuitry we devised for electronic learning.

("Not quite true. If you remember, Tyrrell's motives for modifying the circuits from cognitive to sensory were quite noble. He—")

I know all about it, Pard. . . .

The learning circuit and its sensory variation both had noble beginnings. The original, on which Dalt's patent had only recently expired, had been intended for use by scientists, physicians, and technicians to help them keep abreast of the developments in their sub-or sub-sub-specialties. With the vast amount of research and experimentation taking place across the human sector of the galaxy it was not humanly possible to keep up to date and still find time to put your knowledge to practical use. Dalt's (and Pard's) circuitry supplied the major breakthrough in transmitting information to the cognitive centers of the brain at a rapid rate.

Numerous variations and refinements followed, but Dr. Rico Tyrrell was the first to perfect the sensory mode of transmission. He used it in a drug rehabilitation program to duplicate the sensory effects of addictive drugs, thus weaning his patients psychologically off drugs after their physiological dependence was gone. The idea was quickly pirated, of course, and cassettes were soon available with sensory recordings of fantastic sexual experiences of all varieties.

Giff was whimpering now and flopping around on the floor.

("He's got to be a far-gone button-head to have to tune in at a time like this . . . and right in front of a stranger, at that.")

I understand some of those cassettes are as addictive as Zemmelar and chronic users become impotent in real sexual contexts.

("How come we've never tried one?")

Dalt gave a mental sniff. *I've never felt the need. And when the time comes that I need my head wired so I can get a little—*

There was a groan in the corner: Giff had reached the peak of the recording. His body was arched so that only his palms, his heels, and the back of his skull were in contact with the floor. His teeth were clamped on his lower lip to keep him from crying out. Suddenly he slumped to the floor, limp and panting.

That must be quite a cassette!

("Most likely one of those new numbers that combines simultaneous male and female orgasms—the ultimate in sexual sensation.")

And that's all it is: sensation. There's no emotion involved.

("Right. Superonanism.") Pard paused as they watched their sated guard. ("Do you see what's hanging from his neck?")

Yeah. A flamestone. So?

("So it looks exactly like yours—a cheap imitation, no doubt, but the resemblance is remarkable. Ask him about it.")

Dalt shrugged with disinterest, then noticed Giff stirring. "Are you quite finished?"

The man groggily lifted his slight frame into a sitting position. "I disgust you, don't I," he stated with a low voice, keeping his eyes averted to the floor as he disconnected the cassette from his scalp.

"Not really," Dalt replied, and sincerity was evident in his voice. A few centuries ago he would have been shocked, but he had learned in the interim to view humanity from a more aloof vantage point—a frame of mind he had consciously striven for since his days as The Healer. It had been difficult to maintain at first, but as the years slid by, that frame of mind had become a natural and necessary component of his psyche.

He didn't despise Giff, nor did he pity him. Giff was merely one expression of the myriad possibilities open to human existence.

Dalt moved the gravcuffs downward and seated himself crosslegged on the floor. When Giff had stowed the cassette in a sealed compartment in his overalls, Dalt said, "That's quite a gem you have tied around your neck. Where'd you steal it?"

The fidgety man's eyes flashed uncharacteristically. "It's mine! It may not be real but it's mine. My father gave one to all his children, just as his own mother gave one to him." He held out the stone and gazed at its inner glow.

"Hm!" Dalt grunted. "Looks just like mine."

Giff rose to his feet and approached Dalt. "So you're a Son of The Healer, too?"

"Wha'?"

"The stone . . . it's a replica of the one The Healer wore centuries ago. All Children of The Healer wear one." He was standing over Dalt now and as he reached for the cord around his neck, Dalt idly considered ramming the gravcuff upward into Giff's face.

("That won't work,") Pard warned. ("Even if you did manage to knock him unconscious, what good would it do us? Just play along; I want to hear more about these Children of The Healer.")

So Dalt allowed Giff to inspect his flamestone as he sat motionless. "I'm no Son of The Healer. As a matter of fact, I wasn't aware that The Healer ever had children."

Giff let go of Dalt's gem and let it dangle from its cord again. "Just a figure of speech. We call ourselves his children—great-great-great-*grand*children would be more accurate—because none of us would have been born if it hadn't been for him."

Dalt gave him a blank stare and Giff replied in an exasperated tone, "I'm a descendant of one of the people he cured a couple of hundred years ago. She was a victim of the horrors. And if The Healer hadn't come along and straightened her out, she'd have been institutionalized for all her life; her two sons would never have been born, would never have had children of their own, and so on."

("And you wouldn't be here standing guard over us, idiot!") Pard muttered.

"The first generation of Children of The Healer," Giff went on, "was a social club of sorts, but the group soon became too large and too spread out. We have no organization now, just people who keep his name alive through their families and wear these imitation flamestones. The horrors still strikes everywhere and some say The Healer will return."

"You believe that?" Dalt asked.

Giff shrugged. "I'd like to." His eyes studied Dalt's flamestone. "Yours is real, isn't it?"

Dalt hesitated for an instant, engaged in a lightning conference. *Should I tell him?*

("I think it's our only chance. It certainly won't worsen our situation.")

Neither Pard nor Dalt was afraid of physical violence or torture. With Pard in control of all physical systems, Dalt would feel no pain and could at any time assume a deathlike state with a skin temperature cooled by intense vasoconstriction and cardiopulmonary activity slowed to minimal level.

Yeah. And I'd much prefer getting out of these cuffs and turning a few tables to rolling over and playing dead.

("That would gall me, too. Okay—play it to the hilt.")

"It's real, all right," Dalt told Giff. "It's the original."

Giff's mouth twisted with skepticism. "And I'm president of the Federation."

Dalt rose to his feet, lifting the gravcuff with him. "Your boss is looking for a man who's been alive for two or three centuries, isn't he? Well, I'm the man."

"We know that."

"I'm a man who never sickens, never ages . . . now what kind of a healer would The Healer be if he couldn't heal himself. After all, death is merely the culmination of a number of degenerative disease processes."

Giff mulled this over, accepting the logic but resisting the conclusion. "What about the patch of silver hair and the golden hand?"

"Pull this skullcap off and take a look. Then get some liquor from the cabinet over there and rub it on my left wrist."

After a full minute's hesitation, wherein doubt struggled in the mire of the afterglow of the cassette, Giff accepted the challenge and cautiously pulled the skullcap from Dalt's head. "Nothing! What are you trying—"

"Look at the roots," Dalt told him. "You don't think I can walk around with that patch undyed, do you?"

Giff looked. The roots in an oval patch at the top of Dalt's head were a silvery gray. He jumped away from Dalt as if stung, then walked slowly around him, examining him as if he were an exhibit in a museum. Without a word, he went to the cabinet Dalt had indicated before and drew from it a flask of clear orange fluid.

"I . . . I'm almost afraid to try this," he stammered, opening the container as he approached. He poised the bottle over Dalt's wrists where they were inserted into the gravcuff, hesitated, then took a deep breath and poured the liquor. Most of it splashed on the floor but a sufficient amount reached the target.

"Now rub," Dalt told him.

Without looking up, Giff tucked the flask under his

arm and began to massage the fluid into the skin of Dalt's left wrist and forearm. The liquor suddenly became cloudy and flesh-colored. Giff took a fold of his coveralls and wiped the solution away. From a sharp line of demarcation at the wrist on down over the back of the hand, the skin was a deep, golden yellow.

"You *are* The Healer!" he hissed, his eyes meeting Dalt's squarely for the first time. "Forgive me! I'll open the cuff right now." In his frantic haste to retrieve the key from his coveralls, Giff allowed the liquor flask to slip from beneath his arm and it smashed on the floor.

"Hey! That was real glass!" Dalt said.

Giff ignored the crash and the protest. The key was in his hand and he was inserting it into its slot. The pressure around Dalt's wrists was suddenly eased and as he pulled his hands free, Giff caught the now-deactivated cuff.

"Forgive me," he repeated, shaking his head and fixing his eyes on the floor. "If I'd had any idea that you might be The Healer, I would've had nothing to do with this, I swear! Forgive—"

"Okay! Okay! I forgive you!" Dalt said hurriedly. "Now, do you have a blaster?"

Giff nodded eagerly, reached inside his coveralls, and handed over a small hand model, cheap but effective at close range.

"Good. Now all we've got to do—"

"Hey!" someone yelled from the other side of the room. "What's going on?"

Dalt spun on reflex, his blaster raised. It was Hinter and he had his own blaster ready. There was a flash, then Dalt felt a searing pain as the beam from Hinter's weapon burned a hole through his chest two centimeters to the left of his sternum. As his knees buckled, everything went black and silent.

XII

RUSHING TO THE upper level at the sound of Giff's howl, Kanlos came upon a strange tableau: the prisoner —Dalt, or whatever his name was—was lying on his back with the front of his shirt soaked with blood and a neat round hole in his chest . . . very dead. Giff kneeled over him, sobbing and clutching the empty gravcuff to his abdomen; Hinter stood mutely to the side, blaster in hand.

"You fool!" he screamed, white-faced with rage. "How could you be so stupid!"

Hinter took an involuntary step backward. "He had a blaster! I don't care how valuable a guy is, when he points a blaster in my direction, I shoot!"

Kanlos strode toward the body. "How'd he get a blaster?"

Hinter shrugged. "I heard something break up here and came to investigate. He was out of the cuff and holding the blaster when I came in."

"Explain," he said, nudging the sobbing Giff with his foot.

"He was The Healer!"

"Don't be ridiculous!"

"He was! He proved it to me."

Kanlos considered this. "Well, maybe so. We traced him back to Tolive and that's where The Healer first appeared. It all fits. But why did you let him loose?''

"Because I am a Son of The Healer!'' Giff whispered. "And now I've helped kill him!''

Kanlos made a disgusted face. "Idiots! I'm surrounded by fools and incompetents! Now we may never find out how they kept him alive this long.'' He sighed with exasperation. "All right. We've still got a few rooms left to search.''

Hinter turned to follow Kanlos. "What about him?'' he said, indicating Giff.

"Useless button-head. Forget him.''

They went below, leaving Giff crouched over the body of The Healer.

XIII

("C'MON. WAKE UP!")

Wha' happen?

("Hinter burned a hole right through your heart, my friend.")

Then how come I'm still alive?

("Because the auxiliary heart I constructed in your pelvis a couple of hundred years ago has finally come in handy.")

I never knew about that.

("I never told you. You know how you get when I start making improvements.")

I'll never object again. But what prompted you to build a second heart?

("I've always been impressed by what happened to Anthon when you blasted a hole in his chest, and it occurred to me that it just wasn't safe to have the entire circulatory system dependent on a single pump. So I attached the auxiliary organ to the abdominal aorta, grew a few bypass valves, and let it sit there . . . just in case.")

I repeat: I'll never object again.

("Good. I've got a few ideas about the mineral composition of your bones that I—")

Later. What do we do now?

(We send the button-head home, then we take care of

those two below. But no exertion; we're working on
only one lung.''

How about waiting for them with the blaster?

(''No. Better idea: Remember the sights we came
across in the minds of all those people with the horrors?'')

I've never quite been able to forget.

(''Neither have I, and I believe I can recreate enough
of them to fill this house with a concentrated dose of the
horrors . . . concentrated enough to insure that those
two never bother us or anyone else again.'')

Okay, but let's get rid of Giff.

XIV

WITHOUT WARNING, the body in front of Giff suddenly rolled over and achieved a sitting position. "Stop that blubbering and get out of here," it told him.

Giff's mouth hung open as he looked at the obviously alive and alert man before him with the gory front and the hole in his chest where his heart should be. He looked torn between the urge to laugh with joy and scream with horror. He resolved the conflict by vomiting.

When his stomach had finally emptied itself, he was told to go to the roof, take the emergency chute down to the ground, and keep on going.

"Do not," the body emphasized, "repeat: do not dally around the grounds if you value your sanity."

"But how . . ." he began.

"No questions. If you don't leave now I won't be responsible for what happens to you."

Without another word but with many a backward glance, Giff headed for the roof. At last look, he saw the body climb unsteadily to its feet and walk toward one of the chairs.

Dalt sank into a chair and shook his head. "Dizzy!" he muttered.

("Yeah. It's a long way from the pelvis to the brain. Also, there's some spasm in the aortic arch that I'm having trouble controlling. But we'll be all right.'')

I'll have to trust you on that. When do we start with the horrors?

(''Now. I'll block you out because I'm not sure that even you can take this dose.'')

I was hoping you'd say that, Dalt thought with relief, and watched everything fade into formless grayness.

And from the bloody, punctured body slumped in the chair there began to radiate evil, terror, horror. A malignant trickle at first, then a steady stream, then a gushing torrent.

The men below stopped their search and began to scream.

XV

DALT FINISHED INSPECTING the lower rooms and was fully satisfied that the two gurgling, drooling, blank-eyed creatures that had once been Kanlos and Hinter were no longer a threat to his life and his secret. He walked outside into the cool night air in a vain attempt to soothe his laboring right lung and noticed a form slumped in the bushes.

It was Giff. From the contorted position of his body it was evident that he had fallen from the roof and broken his neck.

"Looks like this Son of The Healer couldn't follow directions," Dalt said. "Must've waited up on the roof and then went crazy when the horrors began and ran over the edge."

("Lot's son.")

"What's that supposed to mean?"

("Nothing. Just a distorted reference to an episode in an ancient religious book,") Pard said, then switched the subject. ("You know, it's amazing that there's actually a cult of Healer-followers awaiting his return.")

"Not really so amazing. We made quite an impression . . . and left a lot undone."

("Not because we wanted to. There was outside interference.")

"Right. But that won't bother us now, with the war going on."

("You want to go back to it, don't you?")

"Yes, and so do you."

("Guess you're right. I'd like to learn to probe a little deeper this time. And maybe find out whoever or whatever's behind the horrors.")

"You've hinted at that before. Care to explain?"

("That's all it is, I'm afraid: a hint . . . a glimpse of something moving behind the scenes. I've no theory, no evidence. Just a gnawing suspicion.")

"Sounds a little farfetched to me."

("We'll see. But first we'll have to heal up this hole in the chest, get the original heart working again—if I may quote you: 'What kind of a healer would The Healer be if he couldn't heal himself!'—and try to think up some dramatic way for The Healer to reappear.")

After a quick change of clothes, they went to the roof and steered their flitter into the night, leaving it to the Meltrin authorities to puzzle out two babbling idiots, a broken button-head, and a respected physicist named Cheserak who had vanished without a trace.

They blamed it on the Tarks, of course.

PART THREE:

Heal thy Nation

YEAR 1231

The horrors persisted at varying levels of virulence for well over a millennium and during that period certain individuals with the requisite stigmata of flamestone, snowy patch of hair, and golden hand, purporting to be The Healer, appeared at erratic intervals. The efforts of these impostors were somehow uniformly successful in causing remissions of the malady. And although this was vigorously dismissed as placebo effect by most medical authorities (with the notable exception of IMC, which, for some unaccountable reason, refused to challenge the impostors), the explanation fell on deaf ears. The Children of The Healer would have none of it. Rational explanations were meaningless to them.

And so the cult grew, inexorably. It crossed planetary, commonwealth, and even racial barriers (we have already discussed the exploits among the Lentemians and among the Tarks during the postwar period), spreading in all directions until . . . the horrors stopped.

As suddenly and as inexplicably as the phenomenon had begun, the horrors came to a halt. No new cases have been reported for the last two centuries and the cult of The Healer is apparently languishing, kept alive only by the fact that various individuals in Healer regalia have been spotted on vid recordings in public places here and there about the planets. (The only consistency noted in regard to these sightings is that, when interviewed later, no one in these scenes could ever remember seeing a man who looked like The Healer.)

The Children of The Healer say that he awaits the day when we shall need him again.

We shall see.

from *The Healer: Man & Myth*

by Emmerz Fent

XVI

FEDERATION CENTRAL: first-adjutant's office, Federation Defense Force.

Ros Petrical paced the room. He was fair, wiry, and prided himself on his appearance of physical fitness. But he wasn't trying to impress the other occupant of his office. That was Bilxer, an old friend and the Federation currency coordinator, who had been passing the time of day when the report came in. Bilxer's department was responsible for tabulating and reporting—for a fee, of course—the fluctuations in the relative values of the member planets' currencies. There had, however, been a distinct and progressive loss of interest in the exchange rates through recent generations of currency coordinators, and consequently Bilxer found himself with a surfeit of time on his hands.

Petrical, until very recently, could hardly complain about being overworked during his tenure as first adjutant. At the moment, however, he wished he had studied finance rather than military science. Then he would be stretched out on the recliner like Bilxer, watching someone else pace the floor.

"Well, there goes the Tark theory," Bilxer said from his repose. "Not that anyone ever truly believed they were behind the incidents in the first place."

"Incidents! That's a nice way of dismissing cold, calculated slaughter!"

Bilxer shrugged off Petrical's outburst as semantic nitpicking. "That leaves the Broohnins."

"Impossible!" Petrical said, flicking the air with his hand. He was agitated, knew it, and cursed himself for showing it. "You heard the report. The survivors in that Tark village—"

"Oh, they're leaving survivors now?" Bilxer interjected. "Must be mellowing."

Petrical glared at his guest and wondered how they had ever become friends. He was talking about the deaths of thousands of rational creatures and Bilxer seemed to assign it no more importance than a minor devaluation of the Tark erd.

Something evil was afoot among the planets. For no apparent reason, people were being slaughtered at random intervals in random locations at an alarming rate. The first incidents had been trifling—trifling, at least, on an interstellar scale. A man burned here, a family destroyed there, isolated settlements annihilated to a man; then the graduation to villages and towns. It was then that reports began to filter into Fed Central and questions were asked. Petrical had painstakingly traced the slaughters, reported and unreported, back over seven decades. He had found no answers but had come up with a number of questions, the most puzzling of which was this: If the marauders wanted to wipe out a village or a settlement, why didn't they do it from the atmosphere? A single small peristellar craft could leave a charred hole where a village had been with little or no danger to the attackers. Instead, they arrived on-planet and did their work with antipersonnel weapons.

It didn't make sense . . . unless terror was part of the object. The attack teams had been very efficient—they had never left a witness. Until now.

"The survivors," Petrical continued in clipped tones, "described the marauders as vacuum-suited humanoids —no facial features noted—appearing out of nowhere amid extremely bizarre atmospheric conditions, and then methodically slaughtering every living thing in sight. Their means of escape? They run toward a certain point and vanish. Granted, the Broohnins are unbalanced as far as ideology goes, but this just isn't their style. And besides, they don't have the technology for such a feat."

"Somebody does."

Petrical stopped pacing. "Yeah, somebody does. And whatever they've got must utilize some entirely new physical principle." He stepped behind his desk and slumped into the seat. His expression was gloomy as he spoke. "The Tarks are demanding an emergency meeting of the General Council."

"Well, it's up to you to advise the director to call one. Do you dare?"

"I don't have much choice. I should have pushed for it some time ago, but I held off, waiting for these slaughters to take on a pattern. As yet, they haven't. But now that the Tarks have been hit, I'm up against the wall."

Bilxer rose and ambled toward the door. "It's fairly commonly accepted that the Federation is dead, a thing of the past. A nice noisy emergency session could lay that idea to rest."

"I'm afraid," Petrical sighed, "that the response to this emergency call will only confirm a terminal diagnosis."

XVII

JOSIF LENDA INVENTORIED the room as he awaited Mr. Mordirak's appearance. The high, vaulted ceiling merged at its edges with row upon row of sealed shelves containing, of all things, books. Must be worth a fortune. And the artifacts: an ornately carved desk with three matching plush chairs, stuffed animals and reptiles from a dozen worlds staring out from corners and walls, interspersed with replicas of incredibly ancient weapons for individual combat . . . maybe they weren't replicas. The room was windowless with dusky indirect lighting and Lenda had that feeling that he had somehow been transported into the dim past.

In spite of—and no doubt because of—his almost pathological reclusiveness, Mr. Mordirak was probably Clutch's best-known citizen. A man of purportedly incredible wealth, he lived in a mansion that appeared to have been ripped out of Earth's preflight days and placed here upon a dizzy pinnacle of stone amid the planet's badlands. As far as anyone could tell, he rarely left his aerie, and when he did so, he demonstrated a remarkable phobia for image recorders of any type.

Lenda felt a twinge of apprehension as he heard a sound on the other side of the pair of wooden doors behind the desk. He desperately needed the aid of a man of Mordirak's stature, but Mordirak had remained studiously aloof from human affairs since the day, nearly a half century ago, when he had suddenly appeared on Clutch. Rumors had flashed then that he had bought the planet. That was highly unlikely, but there grew up about the man an aura of power and wealth that persisted to this day. All Lenda needed was one public word of support from Mordirak and his plans for a seat in the Federation Assembly would be assured.

And so the apprehension. Mordirak never granted interviews, yet he had granted Lenda one. Could he be interested? Or was he toying with him?

The doors opened and a dark-haired, sturdy-looking man of approximately Lenda's age entered. He seated himself smoothly at the desk and locked eyes with the man across from him.

"Why does a nice young man like you want to represent Clutch at the Federation Assembly, Mr. Lenda?"

"I thought I was to see Mr. Mordirak personally," Lenda blurted, and regretted his words as he said them.

"You are," was the reply.

Despite that fact that he had expected him to be older, had expected a more imposing appearance, Lenda had recognized this man as Mordirak from the moment he'd entered the room. The man's voice was young in tone but held echoes of someone long familiar with authority; his demeanor alone had beamed the message to his subconscious instantly, yet the challenge had escaped of its own accord.

"Apologies," he sputtered. "I've never seen an image of you."

"No problem," Mordirak assured him. "Now, how about an answer to that question?"

Lenda shrugged off the inexplicable sensation of inadequacy that this man's presence seemed to thrust upon him and spoke. "I want to be planetary representative because Clutch is a member of the Federation and should have a say in the Assembly. No one here seems to think the Fed is important. I do."

"The Federation is dead," Mordirak stated flatly.

"I beg to differ, sir. Dying, yes. But not dead."

"There has not been a single application for membership in well over three centuries, and more than half of the old members can't stir up enough interest in their populations to send planetary reps, let alone sector reps. I call that *dead*."

"Well, then," Lenda said, jutting out his jaw, "it must be revived."

Mordirak grunted. "What do you want of me?"

"Your support, as I'm sure you are well aware."

"I am politically powerless."

"So am I. But I am also virtually unknown to the populace, which is not true in your case. I need the votes of more than fifty per cent of the qualified citizens of Clutch to send me to Fed Central. To get those votes, all I require is your endorsement."

"You can't get them on your own?"

Lenda sighed. "Last election, I was the only candidate in the running and not even half the qualified population bothered to vote. The Federation Charter does not recognize representatives supported by less than half their constituents."

Mordirak's sudden smile seemed ill-fitted to his face. "Doesn't that tell you something, Mr. Lenda?"

"Yes! It tells me that I need someone who will get them out of their air recliners and over to their vid sets to tap in a simple 'yes' or 'no' during the hour that the polls are open next month!"

"And you think I'm that man?"

"Your name is magic on this planet, Mr. Mordirak. If Clutch's famous recluse thinks representation is important enough to warrant endorsement of a candidate, then the voters will think it important enough to warrant their opinion."

"I'm afraid I can't endorse you," Mordirak said, and his tone held an unmistakable tone of finality.

Lenda tried valiantly to hide his frustration. "Well, if not me, then somebody else. Anyone . . . just to get things moving."

"Sorry, Mr. Lenda, but I've never had much to do with politics and politicians, and I don't intend to begin now.'' He rose and started to turn.

"Damnit, Mordirak!" Lenda cried, leaping to his feet. "The human race is going to hell! We're degenerating into rabble! A group here doing this, a faction there doing that, out-of-touch, smug, indifferent! We've become a bunch of fragments with a common genetic background as our only link. I don't like what I see happening and I want to do something about it!"

"You have passion, Mr. Lenda," Mordirak said with a touch of approval. "But just what is it you think you can do?"

"I . . . I don't know as yet," he replied, cooling rapidly. "First I have to get to Fed Central and work from there—from the inside out. The Federation in its prime was a noble organization with a noble record. I hate to think of it dying of attrition. All the work of men like LaNague and—"

"LaNague . . ." Mordirak murmured as his face softened momentarily "I came of age on his home planet."

"So you're a Tolivian," Lenda said with a sudden nod of understanding. "That would explain your disinterest in politics."

"That's a part of it, yes. LaNague was born on Tolive and is still held in high regard there. And I hold a number of late Tolivians in high regard."

For the first time during their meeting, Lenda felt as if he was talking to a fellow human being. The initial void between them had diminished appreciably and he pressed to take advantage of the proximity. "I visited Fed Central not too long ago. It would break LaNague's heart if he could see—"

"That tactic won't work," Mordirak snapped, and the void reasserted itself.

"Sorry. It's just that I'm at a loss as to what to do."

"I can see that. You're frustrated. You want desperately to be elected but can't even find an election in which to run."

"That's unfair."

"Is it? Why then do you want to go to the seat of

power? 'Born to rule,' perhaps?''

Lenda was silent. He resented the insinuation but it struck a resonance within the bowels of his mind. He had often questioned his political motives and had never been entirely satisfied with the answers. But he refused to accept the portrait Mordirak was painting for him.

"Not to rule," he replied. "If that were my drive, I'd rejoice at the downfall of the Federation. No one ever went to Fed Central to rule unless he was a Restructurist." He paused and averted his eyes. "I'm a romantic, I guess. I've spent most of my adult life studying the Federation and know the way it was in the days before the war. I've seen the old vid recordings of the great debates and decisions. In all sincerity, if you knew the Federation as I know it, and could see it now, you would weep.''

Mordirak remained unmoved.

"And there's another thing," Lenda pressed. "These slaughters, these senseless attacks on random planets, are accelerating. The atrocities are absolutely barbaric in themselves, but I fear the final outcome will be much worse. If the Federation cannot make an adequate response, I foresee the Terran race—in fact, this entire arm of the galaxy—entering a long and perhaps endless period of interstellar feudalism!''

Mordirak's gaze did not flicker. "What is that to me?''

Lenda sagged visibly but made a final attempt to reach him. "Come to Fed Central with me . . . see the decay for yourself.''

"If you wish," Mordirak said. "Perhaps next year.''

"Next year!" Lenda was astounded at his own inability to convey any sense of urgency to the man. "Next year will be too late! The General Council is in emergency session right now.''

Mordirak shrugged. "Today, then. We'll take my tourer.''

In a fog of bewilderment at the turn of events and at Mordirak's total lack of a sense of time, Lenda allowed himself to be led down the dim halls and into the crystalline mountaintop sunlight. They boarded a sporty flitter, lifted, then plunged through the tenuous layer of clouds below on a direct course for the coast. No words were spoken as they set down on the beach and entered a cab in the down-chute of the submarine tube. Their momentum grew slowly until the angle steepened and they shot off the continental shelf toward the bottom of the undersea cavern that held the largest of Clutch's three Haas gates.

The Haas gates had revolutionized interstellar travel a millennium before by allowing ships to enter warp within a star's gravity well. For the first half of their existence, the gates had been placed in interplanetary space. Attempts at operation within a planet's atmosphere had met with tragic results until someone decided to try a deep-pressure method on the ocean floor. It worked. The pressure cushioned the displacement effects and peristellar and interstellar travel was rerevolutionized by eliminating escape-velocity requirements. The orbital gate, however, remained an obvious necessity for incoming craft, since contact with anything other than vacuum at the velocities obtained during warp drive would prove uniformly disastrous.

Lenda said nothing as they entered the sleek tourer, and Mordirak appeared disinclined to break the uncomfortable silence, seemed oblivious to it, in fact. But after the craft had been trundled toward the bronze-hued pillars that represented the gate and had shuddered into warp in the field generated between them, Lenda felt compelled to speak.

"If I may be so bold to ask, Mr. Mordirak, what moved you to change your mind and travel to Fed Central?"

Mordirak, the only other occupant of the tourer's passenger compartment, did not seem to realize he had been spoken to. Lenda waited for what he considered a reasonable period of time and was about to rephrase his question when Mordirak replied.

"I have a horrid fascination for the process of government. I am repulsed by all that it implies and yet I am drawn to discussions and treatises on it. You say the Federation is dying. I want to see for myself." He then leaned back in the seat and closed his eyes.

Further attempts at conversation proved fruitless and Lenda finally resigned himself to silence for the rest of the trip.

After flashing through the Fed Central gate and setting up orbit around the planet, Lenda was unpleasantly surprised at the short wait for seats on the down-shuttle. He muttered his apprehensions.

"The Fed must be in even worse shape than I'd imagined. The call for an emergency session should have crammed the orbits with incoming representatives and the shuttles should be running far behind."

Mordirak nodded absently, lost in his own thoughts.

"From your impassioned description," Mordirak said as they strolled through the deserted, polished corridors of the Assembly Complex, "I half expected to see littered streets and cracked walls."

"Oh, there's decay all right. The cracks are there but they're metaphysical. These halls should be crowded with reporters and onlookers. As it is . . ." His voice trailed off as he caught sight of a dejected-looking figure farther down the corridor.

"I think I know that man," he said. "Mr. Petrical!"

The man looked up but gave no sign of recognition. "No interviews now, I'm afraid."

Lenda continued his approach and extended his hand. "Josif Lenda. We met last year during my clerkship."

Petrical smiled vaguely and murmured, "Of course." After being introduced to Mordirak, who responded with a barely perceptible nod, he turned to Lenda with a grim expression.

"You still sure you want to be a representative?"

"More than ever," he replied. Then, with a glance up and down the deserted corridor, "I only hope there's something left of the Federation by the time I manage to get elected."

Petrical nodded. "That's a very real consideration. Let me show you something." He led them through a door at the far side of the corridor into an enclosed gallery overlooking the huge expanse of the General Council assembly hall. A high podium with six seats was set at the far end of the room. Five of the seats were empty. The lower podium in front of it was designated for sector representatives, and only seven of the forty seats were occupied. The immense floor section belonged to the planetary reps and was virtually deserted. A few lonely figures stood about idly or sat in dejected postures.

"Behold the emergency meeting of the General Council of the Federation of Planets!" Petrical intoned in a voice edged with disgust. "Hear the spirited debates, the clashing opinions!"

There followed a long silence during which the three men looked down upon the tableau, their individual reactions reflected in their faces. Petrical's jaw was thrust forward as his eyes squinted in frustrated anger. Lenda appeared crushed and there was perhaps a trace more fluid in his eyes than necessary for lubrication alone. Mordirak's face was set in its usual mask and only for the briefest instant did a smile twitch at the corners of his mouth.

Finally, Lenda whispered, "It's over, isn't it," and it was a statement, not a question. "Now we begin the long slide into barbarism."

"Oh, it's not really that bad," Petrical began with forced heartiness which faded rapidly as his eyes met Lenda's. There was no sense playing word games with this young man. He knew. "The slide has already begun," he said abruptly. "This just . . ." he waved his hand at the all-but-deserted assembly hall, "just makes it official."

Lenda turned to Mordirak. "I'm sorry I asked you here. I'm sorry I bothered you at all today."

Mordirak looked up from the scene below. "I think it's quite interesting."

"Is that all you can say?" Lenda rasped through his

teeth. He felt sudden rage clutching at his throat. This man was untouchable! "You're witnessing not only the end of the organization that for fifteen hundred years has guided our race into a peaceful interstellar civilization, but the probable downfall of that very civilization as well! And all you can say is it's 'interesting?' "

Mordirak was unperturbed. "Quite interesting. But I've seen enough, I think. Can I offer you transportation back to Clutch?"

"No, thank you," he replied disdainfully. "I'll make my own accommodations."

Mordirak nodded and left the gallery.

"Who was that?" Petrical asked. He knew only the man's name, but fully shared Lenda's antipathy.

Lenda turned back toward the assembly room. "No one."

XVIII

AS HE STEPPED through the lock from the shuttle to his tourer, Dalt considered the strange inner glee that suffused him at the thought of the Federation's downfall. He had seen it coming for a long time but had paid it little heed. In fact, it had been quite some time since he had given much heed at all to the affairs of his fellow humans. Physically disguising himself from them had been a prime concern at one time, but now even that wasn't necessary—a projected psi image of whomever he wished to appear to be proved sufficient in most cases. (Of course, he had to avoid image recorders of any sort, since they were impervious to psi influence.) Humanity might as well be another race, for all the contact he had with it; the symbol of the human interstellar culture, the Federation, was dying and he could not dredge up a mote of regret for it.

And yet, he should feel something for it passing. Five hundred, even two hundred years ago his reactions might have been different. But he had been someone else then and the Fed had been a viable organization. Now, he was Mordirak and the Fed was on its deathbed.

The decline, he supposed, had begun with the termination of the Terro-Tarkan war, a monstrous, seemingly endless conflict. The war had not gone well for the Terrans at first. The monolithic Tarkan Empire had mounted huge assault forces which wrought havoc with

deep incursions into the Terran sphere of influence. But
the monolithism that gave the Tarks their initial advantage proved in the long run to be their downfall.
Their empire had long studied the loose, disorganized,
eccentric structure of the Fed and had read weakness.
But when early victory was denied them and both sides
dug in for a long siege, the diversification of humanity,
long fostered by the LaNague charter, began to tell.

Technological breakthroughs in weaponry eventually
pierced the infamous Tarkan screens and the Emperor
of the Tarks found his palace planet ringed with Terran
dread-naughts. He was the seventh descendant of the
emperor who had started the war, and, true to Tarkan
tradition, he allowed the upper-echelon nobles assem-
bled around him to blast him and his family to ashes
before surrender. Thus honorably ending—in Tarkan
terms—the royal line.

With victory, there followed the expected jubilant
celebration. Half a millennium of war had ended and
the Federation had proved itself resilient and effective.
There were scars, yes. The toll of life from the many
generations involved had reached into the billions and
there were planets on both sides left virtually uninhabi-
table. But the losses were not in resources alone. The
conflict had drained something from the Terrans.

As the flush of victory faded, humanity began to
withdraw into itself. The trend was imperceptible at
first, but it gradually became apparent to the watchers
and chroniclers of the Terran race that expansion had
stopped. Exploratory probes along the galactic perimeter and into the core were postponed, indefinitely.
Extension of the boundaries of Occupied Space slowed
to a crawl.

Man had learned to warp space and had jubilantly
leaped from star to star. He had made mistakes, had
learned from them, and had continued to move on—
until the Terro-Tarkan war. The outward urge had been
stung then and had retreated. Humanity turned inward.
An unvoiced, unconscious directive set the race to tend-
ing its own gardens. The Tarks had been pacified; had,
in fact, been incorporated into the Federation and given

second-class representation. They were no longer a threat.

But what about farther out? Perhaps there was another belligerent race out there. Perhaps another war was in the wings. Back off, the directive seemed to say. Sit tight for a while and consolidate.

But consolidation never occurred, at least not on a productive scale. By the end of the war, the Terrans and their allies were linked by a comprehensive network of Haas gates and were more accessible to one another than ever before. Had the Federation been in the hands of opportunists at that time, a new imperium could have been launched. But the opposite had occurred: Federation officials, true to the Charter, resisted the urge to use the postwar period to extend their franchise over the member planets. They urged, rather, a return to normalcy and worked to reverse the centrist tendencies that all wars bring on.

They were too successful. As requested, the planets loosened their ties with the Federation, but then went on to form their own enclaves, alliances, and commonwealths, bound together by mutual trade and protection agreements. They huddled in their sectors and for all intents and purposes forgot the Federation.

It was this subdividing, coupled with the atrophy of the outward urge, that caused the political scientists the most concern. They foresaw increasing estrangement between the planetary enclaves and, subsequently, open hostility. Without the Federation acting as a focus for the drives and ambitions of the race, they were predicting a sort of interstellar feudalism. From there the race would go one of two ways: complete consolidation under the most aggressive enclave and a return to empire much like the Metep Imperium in the pre-Federation days, or complete breakdown of interstellar intercourse, resulting in barbarism and stagnation.

Dalt was not sure whether he accepted the doomsayers' theories. One thing was certain, however: The Federation was no longer a focus for much of anything anymore.

With the image of the near-deserted General Council

assembly hall dancing in his head, he tried to doze. But a voice as familiar by now as the tone of his own thoughts intruded on his mind.

("Turning and turning in the widening gyre/The falcon cannot hear the falconer;/Things fall apart, the center cannot hold;/mere anarchy is loosed upon the world/. . . the best lose all conviction.")

Don't bother me.

("You don't like poetry, Dalt? That's from one of my favorites of the ancient poets. Appropriate, don't you think?")

I really couldn't care.

("You should. It could apply to your personal situation as well as that of your race.")

Begone, parasite!

("I'm beginning to wish that were possible. You worry me lately. Your personality is disintegrating.")

Spare me your trite analyses.

("I'm quite serious about this. Look at what you've become: a recluse, an eccentric divorced from contact with other beings, living in an automated gothic mansion and surrounding himself with old weapons and death trophies, brooding and miserable. My concern is genuine, though hardly altruistic.")

Dalt didn't answer. Pard had a knack for cutting directly to the core of a matter and this time the resultant exposure was none too pleasant. He had long been plagued by a gnawing fear that his personality was deteriorating. He didn't like what he had become but seemed unable to do anything about it. When and where had the change begun? When had occasional boredom become crushing ennui? When had other people become other things? Even sex no longer distracted him, although he was as potent as ever. Emotional attachments that had once been an easy, natural part of his being had become elusive, then impossible. Perhaps the fact that all such relationships in the past had been terminated by death had something to do with it.

Pard, of course, had no such problems. He did not communicate directly with the world and had never existed in a mortal frame of reference. From the instant he

had gained sentience in Dalt's brain, death had been a
mere possibility, never an inevitability. Pard had no
need of companionship except for occasional chats with
Dalt concerning their dwindling mutual concerns, and
found abstract cogitations quite enthralling. Dalt envied
him for that.

Why, he wondered in a tangent, did he always refer to
Pard in the male gender? Why not "it"? Better yet,
why not "her"? He was wedded to this thing in his head
till death did them part.

("Don't blame your extended lifespan for your present condition,") said the ever-present thoughtrider.
("You're mistaking inertia for ennui. You haven't ex-
hausted your possibilities; in fact, you've hardly dented
them. You adapted well for a full millennium. It's only
in the last one hundred fifty years or so that you've
begun to crack.")

Right again, Dalt thought. Perhaps it had been the
end of the horrors that had precipitated the present
situation. In retrospect, The Healer episodes, for all the
strain they subjected him to, had been high points while
they lasted—crests between shallow troughs. Now he
felt becalmed at sea, surrounded by featureless hori-
zons.

("You should be vitally interested in what is happening to your race, because you, unlike those around you
today, will be there when civilization deteriorates into
feudalism. But nothing moves you. The rough beast of
barbarism is rattling the cage of civilization and all you
can do is stifle a yawn.")

*You certainly are in a poetic mood today. But bar-
barians, like the poor, are always with us.*

("Granted. But they aren't in charge—at least they
haven't been to date. Tell me: Would you like to see a
Federation modeled on the Kwashi culture?")

Dalt found that a jolting vision but replied instead, *I
wish* you *were back on Kwashi!* He instantly regretted
the remark. It was childish and unworthy of him and
further confirmed the deterioration of his mental state.

("If I'd stayed there, you'd be over a thousand years
dead by now.")

"Maybe I'd be happier!" he retorted angrily. There was a tearing sound to his right as the armrest of his recliner ripped loose in his hand.

How'd I do this? he asked.

("What?")

How'd I tear this loose with my bare hand?

("Oh, that. Well, I made some changes a while back in the way the actin and myocin filaments in your striated muscle handle ATP. Human muscle is hardly optimum in that respect. Your maximum muscle tension is far above normal now. Of course, after doing that, I had to strengthen the cross-bridges between the filaments, reinforce the tendinous origins and insertions of the muscles, and then toughen up the joint capsules. It also seemed wise to increase the epidermal keratin to prevent . . .")

Pard paused as Dalt carelessly flipped the ruined armrest onto the cabin floor. In the old days Pard would have received a lecture on the possible dangers of meddling with his host's physiology. Now Dalt didn't seem to care.

("You seriously worry me, Dalt. Making yourself miserable . . . it's unpleasant, but your emotional life is your own affair. I must warn you, however: If you take any action that threatens our physical life, I'll take steps to preserve it—with or without your consent.")

Go away, parasite, Dalt thought sulkily, *and let me nap.*

("I resent your inference. I've more than earned my keep in this relationship. It becomes a perplexing question as to who is really the parasite at this point.")

Dalt made no reply.

Dalt awoke with Clutch looming larger and larger below him as the tourer eased through the atmosphere toward the sea. Amid clouds of steam it plunged into the water and then bobbed to the surface to rest on its belly. A pilot craft surfaced beside it, locked onto the hull, and, as the tourer took on water for ballast, guided it below the surface to its berth on the bottom.

The tube car deposited him on the beach a short time

later and he strolled slowly in the general direction of his flitter. The sun had already completed about a third of its arc across the sky and the air lay warm and quiet and mistily opaque over the coast. Bathers and sunsoakers were out in force.

He paused to watch a little sun-browned, towheaded boy digging in the sand. For how many ages had little boys done that? He knew he must have done the same during his boyhood on Friendly. How long ago was that? Twelve hundred years? It seemed like twelve thousand. He felt as if he had never been young.

He wondered idly if he had made a mistake in refusing to have children and knew immediately that he hadn't. Watching the women he had loved grow old and die had been hard enough; watching his children do the same would have been more than he could have tolerated.

Pard intruded again, this time with a definite tone of urgency. ("Something's happening!")

What're you talking about?

("Don't know for sure, but there's a mammoth psi force suddenly operating nearby.")

A slight breeze began to stir and Dalt glanced up from the boy as he heard excited voices down by the water. The mist in the air was starting to move, being drawn to a point about a meter from the water's edge. A gray, vortical disk appeared, coin-sized at first, then persistently larger. As it grew in size, the breeze graduated to a wind. By the time the disk reached a diameter equal to a man's height, it was sucking in mist and spray at gale force.

Curious, the little boy stood up and began to walk toward the disk, but Dalt put a hand on his shoulder and gently pulled him back.

"Into your sand hole, little man," he told him. "I don't like the looks of this."

The boy's blue eyes looked up at him questioningly but something in Dalt's tone made him turn and crawl back into his excavation.

Dalt returned his attention to the disk. Something about it raised his hackles and he squatted on his haun-

ches to see what would develop. It had stopped growing
now and a number of people, bracing themselves
against the draw of the gale, formed a semicircular
cluster around it at a respectful distance.

Then, as if passing through a solid wall, a vacuum-
suited figure with a blazing jetpack on its back material-
ized and hit the sand at a dead run. Carrying what appeared to be an energy rifle, it swerved to the right and
dropped to one knee. A second figure appeared then,
and as it swerved to the left, the first turned off its jetpack, raised its rifle, and started firing into the crowd.
The second soon joined it and the semicircle of ob-
servers broke into fleeing, terrified fragments. A steady
stream of invaders began to pour onto the beach, fan-
ning out and firing on the run with murderous accuracy.

Dalt had instinctively flattened onto the sand at the
sight of the first invader, and he now watched in horror
as the people who had only moments before been bath-
ing in the sun and the sea became blasted bodies littering
the sand. Panic reigned as scantily clad figures screamed
and scrambled to escape. The marauders, bulky, faceless, and deadly in their vacsuits, pursued their prey
with remorseless efficiency. Their ranks were forty or
fifty strong now and as one ran in his direction, Dalt
realized that he was witnessing and would no doubt
soon be a victim of one of the mindless slaughters Lenda
had been telling him about.

He sensed movement on his right and turned to see
the little boy sprinting across the sand, yelling for his
mother. Dalt opened his mouth to tell him to get down,
but the approaching invader spotted the fleeing figure
and raised his weapon.

Dalt found himself on his feet and racing toward the
invader. With the high quality of marksmanship ex-
hibited by the marauders so far, he knew he had scant
hope of saving the boy. But he had to try. Something,
either concern for a young life or for his own, or a combination of both, made him run. His feet churned up
furious puffs of sand as they fought for traction, but he
could not gain the momentum he needed. The invader's
weapon buzzed quietly and out of the corner of his eye

Dalt saw the boy convulse in mid-stride and go down.

The thought of self-preservation was suddenly submerged in a red tide of rage. Dalt wanted to live, yes. But more than that, right now he wanted to kill. If his pumping feet could get him there in time, the memory of the torn armrest on his tourer told him what he could do. The invader gave a visible start—though no facial expression could be seen through the opaque faceplate —as he caught sight of Dalt racing toward him. He began to swing the blaster around but too late. Dalt pushed the weapon aside, grabbed two fistfuls of the vacsuit fabric over the chest, and pulled. There was a ripping sound, a whiff of fetid air, and then Dalt's hands were inside the suit. They traveled up to the throat and encircled the neck. A dull *snap* followed and the invader went limp.

Extricating his hands, Dalt pushed the body to the ground with one and snatched the falling blaster with the other. After a brief inspection: *How do you work this thing?* There was no trigger.

Beside him, the body of the slain invader suddenly flared with a brief, intolerable, incandescent flash, then oily smoke began to rise from the torn suit.

"What the—" Dalt began out loud, but Pard cut him off.

("A good way to hide your planet of origin. But never mind that. Try that little button on the side of the stock and try it quickly. I believe you've drawn some unwanted attention to yourself.")

Dalt glanced around and saw one of the invaders staring at him, momentarily stunned with amazement. Then he began to raise his weapon into the firing position.

Suddenly everything slowed, as if under water.

What's going on?

("I've accelerated your mind's rate of perception to give you a much-needed edge over the energy bolt that's about to come our way.")

The blaster had inched up to the invader's shoulder by now and Dalt dove to his left. He seemed to float gracefully, gently through the air. But there was nothing gentle about his impact with the ground. He grunted, rolled, pointed his blaster in the general direction of the invader, and pressed the button three times in rapid succession.

One of the energy bolts must have found its mark. The invader threw up his arms in a slow, wide arc and drifted toward the sand to rest on his back.

Then, as movements resumed their normal cadence, the body flared and belched smoke like the one before it. Dalt noted that he now occupied a position behind the advancing line of marauders.

Maybe you'd better keep up the speed on the perception, he told Pard.

("I can only do it in bursts. The neurons can't maintain the necessary metabolic rate for more than a minute or two.")

Dalt settled himself in the prone position, shouldered the weapon, and found that the button fit under his thumb with only a little stretching.

Let's even up the odds a little while we can. Without the slightest hesitation or remorse, he sighted on the unsuspecting backs of the invaders as they went on with their slaughter of the remaining bathers. As the invaders fell one by one to the silent bolts of energy from Dalt's weapon, the skills he had learned as a game hunter on the lesser-settled planets of Occupied Space came back to him: Hit the stragglers and the ones on the perifery, then move inward. A full dozen of their comrades lay dead and smoking on the sand before the main body of the force realized that all was not going according to plan.

A figure in the center of the rank looked around and, noticing that his detail was unaccountably shrinking in size, signaled to the others. They began to turn their attention from the bathers before them to seek out the unexpected threat from the rear. Pard accelerated perception again and then Dalt's weapon began to take a merciless toll of the force. He was constantly moving and sighting the strange blaster, getting the feel of it and becoming more deadly with every bolt he fired. As soon as an invader raised his weapon in his direction, he would shift, sight, and fire, shift-sight-fire, shift-sight-fire. If the muscles of his fingers, arms, and shoulders could have responded at the speed of his perception, he would have killed them all by now. As it was, he had cut their number in half. The assault had been effectively crippled and it wouldn't take many more casualties before it would fall apart completely.

As Dalt sighted on the figure he took to be the leader, his vision suddenly blurred and vertigo washed over him. The wave receded briefly, then pounded down upon him again with greater force. He felt a presence, totally malignant, totally alien . . . and yet somehow oddly familiar.

Then came an indescribable wrenching sensation and he felt for an instant as if he were looking at the entire universe from both within and without. Then he saw and felt nothing.

He awoke with sand in his eyes and nostrils and the murmur of the sea and human voices in his ears. Rising to his knees, he brushed the particles from his face with an unsteady hand and opened his eyes.

A small knot of people encircled him, its number growing steadily. The circle widened as he gained his feet. All eyes were fixed upon him, and mixed among the hushed mutterings of the voices, the word "Healer" was repeated time and again. It was suddenly obvious that his psi cover must have cut off while he was unconscious.

Dalt felt something in his right hand: the stolen weapon. He loosened his grip and let it fall to the sand. As he resumed the interrupted trek to his flitter, the crowd parted and left him a wide path obstructed only by the bodies of fallen bathers and the remains of the invaders he had killed.

He surveyed the scene as he walked. The assault had apparently been broken: the attackers were gone, their vortical gateway from who-knows-where had closed. The still-smoldering ashes of the invaders who had not escaped gave him a primitive sense of satisfaction.

That'll teach 'em.

The crowd followed him to his flitter at a respectful

distance and stood gazing upward as he piloted the craft above the mist and toward the mountains. Reaction began to set in and his hands were shaking when he reached the aerie. Gaining the study, Dalt poured himself a generous dose of the thin, murky Lentemian liquor he had acquired a taste for in the last century or so. He usually diluted it, but took it straight now and it burned delightfully all the way down.

Sitting alone in the darkness with his feet on the desk, Dalt became aware of a strange sensation. No, it wasn't the liquor. It was something else . . . something unpleasant. He put the glass down and returned his feet to the floor as he recognized the feeling.

He was alone.

Pard? he called mentally, awaiting the familiar reply. None came.

He was on his feet now and using his voice. "Pard!"

The emptiness that followed was more than a lack of response. There was a void within.

Pard was gone. Pard the father, Pard the son, Pard the wife and mother, Pard the mentor, the confidant, the companion, the preserver, the watchdog, Pard the friend, Pard . . . was gone.

The sudden shattering sensation of being alone for the first time in over a millennium was augmented by the awareness that without Pard he was no longer immortal. The weight of the centuries he had lived became crushing as Dalt realized that once again his days could be numbered.

His voice rose to a scream.

"Pard!"

XIX

THREE SULLEN DAYS passed, during which Dalt's aerie was besieged by a legion of news-service reporters vying for an interview. The Healer had returned and everyone wanted an exclusive. Foreseeing this, Dalt had hired a security force to keep them all away. Finally word came that a Federation official and a local politico named Lenda were requesting an audience, claiming they were acquaintances. Should they be allowed in?

Dalt nodded to the face on the screen and switched off the set. *What do they want?* he wondered. If it was a return of The Healer, they were out of luck. Without Pard he had no special psionic powers; he was just another man, and a strange-looking one at that.

It really didn't matter what they wanted. Dalt, strangely enough, wanted some company. For three days he had sulked in the windowless study, and an unaccustomed yearning for sunlight, fresh air, and other human beings had grown within him.

The door to the study opened and Lenda entered with Petrical following. Wonder and awe were evident on the former's face as he remembered the last time he'd been in this room. He had sat across the desk from another man then—at least it had seemed like another man. Now, a thousand-year legend sat before him. The white patch of hair atop his head and the golden hand—only the flamestone was missing—accentuated an image known to every being in Occupied Space. Petrical seemed less impressed but his manner was reserved.

"Nice to see you two gentlemen again," Dalt said with pointed cordiality, fixing his eyes on Lenda. "Please sit down."

They did so with the awkward movements of outlanders in a strange temple. Neither spoke.

"Well?" Dalt said finally. Four or more days ago he would have waited indefinitely, enjoying their discomfiture at the long silence. Now he was possessed of a sense of urgency. Minutes were precious again.

Petrical gained his voice first but fumbled with titles. "Mr. Mordirak . . . Healer . . ."

"Dalt will do nicely."

"Mr. Dalt, then." Petrical smiled with relief. "There's one question I must ask you, for my own sake if not for humanity's: Are you really The Healer?"

Dalt paused, considering his answer. Then, "Does it really matter?"

Furrows appeared on Petrical's brow but Lenda straightened in his chair with sudden comprehension.

"No, it doesn't." He glanced at Petrical. "At least not for practical purposes. By now most of Occupied Space considers him The Healer and that's all that matters. Look what happened: A lone man, outnumbered fifty to one, turns back a murderous assault on helpless bathers. And that man happens to look exactly like The Healer. The incident has proven more than enough for the Children of The Healer and I believe it is quite enough for me."

"But how could you be The—" Petrical blurted, but Dalt stopped him with an upraised hand.

"That is not open for discussion."

Petrical shrugged. "All right. We'll accept it as our basic premise and work from there."

"To where?"

"That will be entirely up to you, Mr. Dalt," Lenda said.

"Yes. Entirely." Petrical nodded, taking the lead.

"You may or may not be aware of what has been taking place during the last three standard days. Federation Central has been bombarded with requests for information on the Clutch incident from all corners of Occupied Space. The isolated slaughters which until three days ago had been of interest only to the victim planets—and even in those cases of only passing interest—are fast becoming a major concern. Why? Because the Children of The Healer, a group that has previously been of mere sociological interest because of its origin and its sheer size—and long thought defunct—has undergone a tremendous resurgence and is applying political pressure for the first time in its history."

Dalt frowned. "I never knew they were still around in any number."

"Apparently the group never died out; it just became less visible. But they've been among us all along, keeping to themselves, growing and passing along the article of faith that The Healer would one day return in time of crisis and they should be ready to aid him by whatever means necessary."

"I'm gratified," Dalt said quickly, "but please get to the point."

"That *is* the point," Lenda said. "People in and around Fed Central have recognized these assaults as the first harbinger of interstellar barbarism. They see a real threat to our civilization but have been powerless to do anything about it—as you well know. They could no longer find a common thread among the planets. But the thread was there all along: your followers. The Children of The Healer form an infrastructure that cuts across all boundaries. All that was needed was some sort of incident—'sign,' if you will—to activate them, and you provided it down there on the beach. You, as The Healer, took a stand against the butchery of these assaults, and that suddenly makes opposition to them a cause for your followers."

"They're working themselves up to a frenzy," Petrical added, "but totally lack direction. I sent representatives from the Federation Defense Force with offers of cooperation, but they were uniformly rebuffed."

"That leaves me, I suppose," Dalt said.

Petrical sighed. "Yes. Just say the word and we can turn a rabble into a devoted, multicentric defense force."

"Blasterfodder, you mean."

"Not at all. The civilians have been blasterfodder for these assaults to date. They're the ones being slaughtered and they're the ones we want to protect."

"Why don't they just protect themselves?" Dalt asked.

"First off, they're not set up for it. Secondly, the assaults take place in such a limited area when they hit that there's a prevailing attitude of 'it can't happen here.' That will eventually change if the number of assaults continues to rise at its present rate, but by then it may be too late. The biggest obstacle to organizing resistance remains our inability to name the enemy."

"Weren't there any clues left down on the beach?"

Petrical shook his head. "Nothing. The bodies were completely incinerated. All we know about the marauders is that they're carbon-cycle beings and either human or markedly humanoid. The weapons they carried had a lot of alien features about them, but that could be intentional." He grunted. "A bizarre transport system, strange weapons, and bodies that self-destruct . . . someone's trying awfully hard to make this look like the work of some new alien race. But I don't buy it. Not yet."

Dalt shifted in his chair. "And what do you expect me to do about all this?"

"Say a few words to the leaders of the planetary Healer sects," Petrical replied. "We can bring them here or to Fed Central or wherever you'd like. All we have to tell them is they'll see The Healer in person and they'll come running."

"And what's in all this for you?"

"Unity. We can perhaps go a step further beyond a coordinated defense. Perhaps we can bind the planets together again, start a little harmony amid the discord."

"And inject a little life into the Federation again," Lenda added.

Dalt turned on him, a touch of the old cynicism in his voice. "That would make you the man of the hour, wouldn't it?"

Lenda reddened. "If you harbor any doubts about my motives which might prevent you from acting, I will withdraw myself completely from the picture."

Dalt was beginning to see Josif Lenda in a new light. Perhaps this errant politician had the makings of a statesman. The two species were often confused, although the former traditionally far outnumbered the latter. He smiled grimly. "I don't think that will be necessary."

Lenda looked relieved but Petrical frowned. "Somehow I don't find your tone encouraging."

Dalt hesitated. He didn't want to turn them down too abruptly but he had no intention of allowing himself to become involved in another conflict like the Terro-Tarkan war, which this might well escalate to in the near future. He still had a number of good years left—in normal human terms—but to a man who had become accustomed to thinking in terms of centuries, it seemed a terribly short number. He knew that should the coming struggle last only half as long as the T-T war, any contribution he made, no matter how exalted the expectations of the two men before him, would be miniscule. And besides, he had things to do. Just what those things were he had yet to decide, but the remaining years belonged to him alone and he intended to be miserly with them, milking them for every drop of life they held.

"I'll think about it," he told them, "and give you my decision in a few days."

Lenda's lips compressed but he said nothing. Petrical gave out a resigned sigh and rose. "I suppose we'll just have to wait, then."

"Right," Dalt said, rising. "One of the security men will show you out."

As the dejected pair exited, Dalt was left alone to face

a chaotic jumble of thoughts and emotions. He paced the room in oppressive solitude. He felt guilty and didn't know why. It was his life, wasn't it? He hadn't wanted to be a messiah; it had been manufactured for him. He'd only wanted to perform a service. Why should he now be burdened with the past when the future seemed so incredibly short?

His thoughts turned to Pard, as they had incessantly for the past three days. It was obvious now that their two minds had been in tandem far too long; the sudden severing of the bond was proving devastating. He did not feel whole without Pard—he was a gelding, an amputee.

He felt anger now—inwardly at his own confusion, outwardly at . . . what? At whatever had killed Pard. Someone or something had taken a part of him down on that beach. The mind with which he had shared twelve hundred years of existence, shared like no other two minds had ever shared, had been snuffed out. The anger felt good. He fueled it: Whoever or whatever it was that had killed Pard would have to pay; such an act could not be allowed to pass without retribution.

He leaped to the vidcom and pressed the code for the guard station. "Have those two men left the property yet?" he demanded.

The security chief informed him that they were at the gate now.

"Send them back."

"The pattern of these attacks is either inapparent at this time," Petrical was saying, "or there simply is no pattern." He was in his element now, briefing the leaders of the planetary sects of the Children of The Healer.

Dalt watched the meeting on a vid panel in the quarters that had been set up for him on Fed Central. As The Healer, he had appeared before the group a few minutes ago, speaking briefly into the awed silence that had filled the room upon his arrival. It continued to amaze him that no one questioned his identity. His resemblance to the millions and millions of holos of The Healer in homes throughout Occupied Space was, of course, perfect. But that could be achieved by anyone willing to sink some money into reconstructive work. No . . . there was more to it than appearance. They seemed to sense that he was the genuine article. More importantly, they *wanted* him to be The Healer. Their multigenerational vigil had been vindicated by his return.

A few words from The Healer emphasizing the importance of organized resistance to the assaults and endorsing cooperation with the Federation had been sufficient. Petrical would take it from there.

The plan was basically simple and would probably prove inadequate. But it was a start. The Children of The Healer would form a nucleus for planetary militia forces which would be on day-and-night standby. At the first sighting of a vortex, or as soon as it was known that there was an attack in progress, they were to be notified and would mobilize immediately. Unless a local or planetary government objected, representatives from the Federation Defense Force would be sent out to school them in tactics. The main thrust of this would be to teach the first group on the scene how to cut the invaders off from their passage until other groups could arrive and a full counteroffensive could be undertaken.

The Children of The Healer would become minutemen, a concept of defense that had been lost in the days of interstellar conflict.

The sect leaders would leave by the end of the day. After that it would be a waiting game.

"I just got word that you were back," Petrical said as he entered Dalt's quarters. His features showed a mixture of relief and annoyance at the sight of Dalt. "You're free, of course, to come and go as you please, but I wish you'd let someone know before you disappear like that again. Nine days without a word . . . we were getting worried."

"I had a few private sources of information to check

out," Dalt said, "and I had to do it in person."

"What did you learn?"

Dalt threw himself into a lounger. "Nothing. No one even has a hint of who or what's behind all this. Anything new at this end?"

"Some good news, some not so good," Petrical replied, finding himself a seat. "We've had reports of four assaults in the past eight days. The first two occurred on planets which had not yet set up battle-ready militia units. The third"—his face broke into a smile—"occurred in a recreational area on Flint!"

Dalt began to laugh. "Oh, I'd have given anything to be there! What happened?" Flint was an independent planet, a former splinter world on which virtually every inhabitant was armed and ready to do battle.

"Well, we don't have much hard information—you know how the Flinters are about snoopers—but all reports indicate that the assault force was completely wiped out." He shook his head in grudging admiration. "You know, I've always thought that everyone on Flint was a little crazy, but I'll bet it's quite some time before they're bothered with one of these assaults again."

"What about the minutemen?" Dalt asked. "Have they seen any action?"

Petrical nodded. "Yesterday, on Aladdin. A vortex was reported only a hundred kilometers away from a fledgling unit. They didn't do too well. They forgot all their tactical training. Granted, it wasn't much, but they might as well have had none at all for the way they conducted the counterattack. They forgot all about cutting off the escape route; just charged in like crazy men. A lot of them were killed, but they did manage to abort the attack."

"First blood," Dalt said. "It's a start."

"Yes, it is," Petrical agreed. He glanced up as Lenda hurried into the room but kept on speaking. "And as the militia groups proliferate I think we can contain these attacks and eventually render them ineffective. When that happens, we'll just have to wait and see what response our unknown assailants make to our counter-measures.''

"They've already made it," Lenda said in a breath-less voice. "Neeka was just hit simultaneously in four different areas! The militia groups didn't know which way to go. The attacks were all in greater force than previous ones and the carnage is reported as incredi-ble." He paused for reaction and found it in the grim, silent visages of the two men facing him. "There was an unusual incident, however," he continued. "One of the minutemen drove a lorry flitter into the vortex."

Dalt shook his head sadly. "I guess our side has it suicidal elements, too."

"Why do you say that?" Lenda asked.

"Because the passage obviously has either low or no pressure on the other side of the opening. It appears to be a vortex because the pressure differential sucks in at-mosphere wherever it opens. The attackers don't wear jetpacks and vacsuits just to hide their identity. I'm sure they *must* wear them to survive transit through the passage."

Petrical nodded in agreement. "We've assumed that from the beginning, and have told the men to keep their distance from the vortex. That fool's bodily fluids prob-ably started to boil as soon as he crossed the threshold."

"But it's indicative of the dedication of these groups that they all want to try the same stunt now," Lenda said. "They want to carry the battle to the enemy."

"A counterattack on the enemy's home position would be the answer to many problems," Petrical mused, "but where is their home? Until we find out, we're just going to have to use the forces we've got to play a holding game." He glanced across the room. "Any ideas, Mr. Dalt?"

"Yes. A couple of obvious ones, and one perhaps not so obvious. First, we must definitely discourage the minutemen from entering the passage. Next, we've got to expand the militia groups. These attacks are escalat-ing rapidly. Rather than random incidents, they're now occurring with a murderous regularity that worries me. This whole affair could be bigger and more sinister than anyone—and that includes the two of you—has yet appreciated."

"I'm ahead of you on that last point," Petrical said with a satisfied air. "Before coming in here I issued another call for an emergency session of the General Council, and this time I think the response will be different. Your followers have been agitating for action on all the planets and have generated real concern. As a result, the Federation has received a steady stream of applications for reinstatement. In fact, there are loads of fresh new representatives on their way to Fed Central right now."

This was not news to Lenda, who kept his eyes on Dalt. "What's your 'not so obvious' idea?"

"Drone flitters equipped with reconnaissance and signal gear," he replied. "They've given us a tunnel right to their jump-off point. Why don't we use it against them? The flitters can send out a continual subspace beam and we can set up an all-points directional watch to see where they end up."

Petrical jumped to his feet. "Of course! We can place a drone with each militia group and it can send it through during a counterattack. We'll keep sending them through until we've pinpointed their position. And when we know where to find them . . ." He paused. "Well, they've got a lot of lives to answer for."

"Why can't we just send an attack force through?" Lenda asked.

"Because we wouldn't know where we'd be sending them," Petrical replied. "We don't know a thing about this vortical passage. We assume it to be a subspace tunnel, but we don't know. If it is, then we're dealing with a technology that dwarfs anything we have. Any man who got through to the other end—and that's a big "if" in itself—would probably be killed before he had a chance to look around. No. Unmanned craft first."

Lenda persisted. "How about sending a planetary bomb through?"

"Those have been outlawed by convention, haven't they?" Dalt said.

Petrical gazed at the floor. "A few still exist." He glanced up. "They're in deep-space hidey holes, of course. But a planetary bomb is out of the question. We'd have to manufacture a lot more of them, one for every planet involved, and they'd have to be armed and trundled to the assault scene by inexperienced personnel. A tragedy of ghastly proportions would be inevitable. We'll stick with Mr. Dalt's idea."

The two men left hurriedly, leaving Dalt alone with a feeling of satisfaction. It was gratifying to have his idea accepted so enthusiastically, an idea that was totally his. He had relied too much on Pard's computer-speed analyses in recent centuries. It felt good to give birth to an idea again. The lines between his own mental processes and Pard's had often blurred and it had at times been difficult to discern where an idea had originated.

With the thought of Pard, a familiar presence seemed to waft through the room and touch him.

"Pard?" he called aloud, but the sensation was gone. An old memory and nothing more.

Pard, he thought as he clenched his golden hand into a fist before his eyes. *What did they do to you, old friend?*

XX

THERE WAS AN awful wrenching sensation, at once numbing and excruciatingly painful, and then Pard's awareness expanded at a cataclysmic rate. The beach was left behind, as were Clutch and its star, then the entire Milky Way, then all the galaxies.

He had been cut free from Dalt. He had no photoreceptors, yet he could see; he had no vibratory senses, and yet he could hear. He was now pure, unhindered awareness. He soared giddily, immaterially. Spatial relationships were suddenly meaningless and he was everywhere. The universe was his . . .

. . . or was it?

He felt a strain . . . subtle at first but steadily growing more pronounced . . . a stretching of the fibers of his consciousness . . . thoughts were becoming fuzzy . . . he was becoming disoriented. The tension of cosmic awareness was rapidly becoming unbearable as the infinite scope and variety of reality threatened to crush him. All the worlds, all the lifeforms, and all the vast empty spaces in between pressed upon him with a force that threatened sudden and irrevocable madness. He had to focus down . . .

focus down . . .

focus down . . .

He was on the beach again. Dalt lay sprawled on the

sand, alive but unconscious. Pard watched as the marauders made a hasty retreat toward their hole in space. The question of their identity still piqued his curiosity and he decided to find out where they were going. Why not? Dalt was safe and he was gloriously free to follow his whims to the ends of existence.

He hesitated. The bond that had united their minds for twelve centuries was broken . . . but other bonds remained. It would be strange, not having Dalt around. He found the indecision irritating and steeled himself to go.

("Goodbye, Steve,") Pard finally said to the inert form he had suddenly outgrown. ("No regrets, I hope.") His awareness shifted toward the closing vortex. Like a transformed chrysalis departing its cocoon, he left Dalt behind.

Within the vortex he found the deadly silence of complete vacuum and recognized the two-dimensional grayness of subspace. The attackers activated their propulsion units and seemed to know where they were going. Pard followed.

Abruptly, they passed into real space again, onto a beach not unlike the one on Clutch. There was no mist here, however. The air was dry and clear under a blazing sun that Pard classed roughly as GO. There were other differences: The dunes had been fused and were filled with machinery for kilometers in either direction up and down the coast, and more was under construction.

He turned his attention to the inhabitants of the beach. As the remnant of the assault force landed on the beach, each member stripped off his or her vacsuit and bowed toward a mass of rock on the sea's horizon.

They were most definitely not human, nor did they belong to any race Pard had ever seen. He allowed his awareness to expand to locate his position relative to Occupied Space. The discovery was startling.

He was in the far arm of the Milky Way, beyond the range of even the deepest human probe, sixty thousand light-years away from the edge of Occupied Space. And yet the attackers had traversed the distance with little more than a jet-assisted flying leap into subspace. The ability to extend a warp to such a seemingly impossible degree, from atmosphere to atmosphere with pinpoint accuracy, indicated a level of technological sophistication that was frightening.

He focused down again and allowed his awareness to drift through the worlds of these beings. They were oxygen breathers and humanoid with major and minor differences. On the minor side was the lack of a nose, which was replaced by a single oblong, vertical olfactory orifice. A major variation was the presence of two accessory appendages originating from each axilla. These were obviously vestigial, being supported internally by cartilage and equipped with only minute amounts of atrophic muscle. Both sexes—another minor variation here was the placement of male gonads within the pelvis —adorned the appendages with paints and jewelry.

After observing a small, hivelike community for a number of local days, he concluded that from all outward appearances, this was a quiet and contented race. They laughed, cried, loved, hated, fought, cheated, stole, bought, sold, produced, and consumed. The children played, the young adults courted and eventually married—the race was strictly monogamous—had more children, took care of them, and were in turn cared for when age made them feeble.

A seemingly docile people. Why were they crossing an entire galaxy to slaughter and maim a race that didn't even know they existed?

Pard searched on, focusing on world after world. He found their culture to be oppressively uniform despite the fact that it spanned an area greater than that of the Federation and the old Tarkan Empire combined. He came upon the ruins of three other intelligent races they had contacted. These races had not been assimilated, had not been subjugated, had not been enslaved. They had been annihilated. Every last genetic trace had been obliterated. Pard recoiled at the incongruous racial ferocity of these creatures and searched on for a reason. The most consistent feature of the culture was the ubiquitous representation of the visage of a member of their own race. A holo of it was present in every room of every hive and a large bust occupied a traditional corner of the main room. There were huge bas-reliefs protruding from the sides of the buildings and carved heads overhanging the intersections of major thoroughfares. The doorways to the temples in which one fifth of every day was spent in obeisant worship were formed in the shape of the face. The faithful entered through the mouth.

And there in the temples, perhaps, was a clue to the mysterious ferocity of this race. The rituals were intricate and laborious but the message came through: "We are the chosen ones. All others offend the sight of the Divine One."

Pard expanded again and refocused on the mother world, his port of entry, the planet from which the attacks were launched. He noted that there was now a much larger contingent of troops on the beach: they were bivouacked in half a dozen separate areas.

Multiple attacks? he wondered. Or a single massive one? He realized he had lost all track of time and his thoughts strayed to Steve. Was he all right or had he been caught in another attack? It was highly unlikely but still a possibility.

He vacillated between investigating that revered mound of rock in the sea and checking on Dalt. The former was a curiosity; the latter, he realized, would soon become a compulsion.

Had he possessed lungs and vocal cords, he would have sighed as he expanded to encompass the entire Milky Way; he then allowed a peculiar homing instinct to guide him to Steven Dalt, who was sitting alone in a small room on Fed Central.

He watched him for a few moments, noting that he seemed to be in good health and good spirits. Then Dalt suddenly sat erect. "Pard?" he called. He had somehow sensed his presence and Pard knew it was time to leave again.

Back on the alien mother world, he concentrated on his previous target—the island. It was immediately evident that this was not a natural formation but an artifact cut out of the mainland and set upon a ridge on the ocean floor. The island was a single huge fortress-temple shaped in the form of what he now knew to be the face of the race's goddess; the structures upon it formed the features of the face. An altogether cyclopean feat of engineering.

He allowed his awareness to flow down wide, high-ceilinged corridors tended by guards armed with bows and spears—an insane contrast to the troops gathered on the mainland. The corridors were etched with the history of the race and its godhead. In an instant, Pard knew all of the goddess's past, knew what she had been to humanity and what she had planned for it. He knew her. Even had a name for her. They had met . . . thousands of times.

He sank deeper into the structure and came across banks of sophisticated energy dampers—that explained the primitive weapons on the guards. Rising to sea level again, he found himself within a tight-walled maze and decided to see where it led.

He finally found her at the very heart of the edifice, in a tiny room at the end of the maze. Her body was pale, corpulent, and made only minimal voluntary movements. But she was clean and well cared for—a small army of attendants saw to that.

She was old, nearly as old as mankind itself. A genetic freak with a cellular consciousness much like Pard had possessed when in Steve's body, which had kept her physically alive and functioning over the ages. Unlike Dalt/Pard, however, the goddess had only one consciousness, but that was a prodigious one, incorporating psionic powers of tremendous range through which she had dominated her race for much of its existence, shaping its goals and fueling its drives until they had merged and became one with her will.

Unfortunately, the goddess had been a full-blown

psychotic for the past three thousand years.

She hated and feared anything that might question her divine supremacy. That was why three other races had already perished. She even distrusted her own worshipers, had made them move her ancient temple out to sea and insisted that her guards don the garb and accouterments of the days of her girlhood.

Pard was aghast at the scope of the tragedy before him. Here was a race that had color and variety in its past. Now, however, through the combination of a psionically augmented religion and a philosophy of racial supremacy, it had been turned into a hive of obedient drones with their lives and culture centered around their goddess-queen. Any independent minds born into the race were quickly culled out once they betrayed their unorthodox tendencies. The reasoning was obvious: The will of the goddess was more than the law of the land—it was divine in origin. To question was heresy; to transgress was sacrilege. The result was a corrupt version of natural selection on an intellectual level. The docile mind that found comfort in orthodoxy survived and thrived, while the reasoner, the questioner, the wavemaker, the rebel, the iconoclast, and the skeptic became endangered species.

As Pard watched her, the goddess lifted her head and opened her eyes. A line about "a gaze blank and pitiless as the sun" went through his mind. She sensed his scrutiny. Her psi abilities made her aware of his presence, tenuous as it was.

She threw a thought at him. It was garbled, colored with rage, couched in madness, but the context could be approximated as:

You again! I thought I had destroyed you!

Enjoying her impotent anger, Pard wished he had the power to send a laugh pealing through the chamber to further arouse her paranoia. As it was, he'd have to be content with observing her thrashing movements as she tried to pinpoint his location.

Pard's awareness began to expand gradually and he soon found himself around as well as within the temple.

He tried to focus down again but was unable to do so. He continued to expand at an accelerated rate. He was encircling the planet now.

For the first time since he had awakened to sentience in Dalt's brain, Pard knew fear. He was out of control. Soon his consciousness would be expanded and attenuated to the near-infinite limits he had experienced immediately after being jolted from Steve's body—permanently. And he knew that would be the end of him. His mind would never be able to adjust to it; his intelligence would crumble. He'd end up a nonsentient life force drifting through eternity. It had long been theorized that consciousness could not exist without a material base. He had proven that it could—but not for long. He had to set up another base. He tried desperately to enter the mind of one of the goddess's subjects but found it closed to him. The same with the lower lifeforms.

All minds were closed to him . . . except perhaps one. . . .

He headed for home.

XXI

DALT AWOKE WITH a start and bolted upright in bed.

("Hello, Steve.")

A cascade of conflicting emotions ran over him: joy and relief at knowing Pard was alive and at feeling whole again, anger at the nonchalance of his return. But he bottled all emotions and asked, *What happened? Where've you been?*

Pard gave him a brief but complete account in the visual, auditory, and interpretive mélange possible only with mind-to-mind communication. When it was over, it almost seemed to Dalt that Pard had never been gone. There were a few subtle differences, however.

Do you realize that you called me "Steve"? You've been addressing me by my surname for the last century or so.

("You seem more like the old Steve.")

I am. Immortality can become a burden at times, but facing the alternative for a while is a sobering experience.

("I know,") Pard replied, remembering the panic that had gripped him before he had managed to regain the compact security of Dalt's mind. They were now welded together—permanently.

"But back to the matter at hand," Dalt said aloud. "You and I now know what's behind these assaults. The

question that bothers me most is: Why us? I mean, if
she wants to send her troops out to kill, surely there are
other races closer to her than sixty thousand light-
years."

("Perhaps the human mind is especially sensitive to
her, I don't know. Who can explain a deranged mind?
And believe me, this one is deranged! She's blatantly
paranoid with xenophobia, delusions of grandeur, and
all the trappings. Steve, this creature actually believes
she is divine! It's not a pose with her. And as far as her
race is concerned, she is god.")

"Pity the atheist in a culture like that."

("There are none! How can there be? When these
beings speak of their deity, they're not referring to an
abstraction or an ephemeral being. Their goddess is in-
carnate! And she's with them everywhere! She can
maintain a continuous contact with her race—it's not
control or anything like that, but a hint of *presence*. She
has powers none of them possess *and she doesn't die!*
She was with them when they were planet-bound, she
was with them when they made their first leap into
space. She has guided them throughout their entire
recorded history. It's not a simple thing to say 'no' to all
that.")

"All right, so she's divine as far as they're concerned,
but how can she change an entire race into an army of
berserk killers? She must have some sort of mind control."

("I can see you have no historical perspective on the
power of religion. Human history is riddled with
atrocities performed in the names of supposedly benign
gods whose only manifestations were in books and
tradition. This creature is not merely a force behind her
culture . . . she *is* her culture. Her followers attack and
slaughter because it is divine will.")

Dalt sighed. "Looks like we're really up against the
wall. We were planning to send probes through the
passages to try to locate the star system where the
assaults originate so we could launch a counteroffensive. Now it makes no difference. Sixty thousand light-

years is an incomprehensible distance in human terms. If there was just some way we could get to her, maybe we could give her a nice concentrated dose of the horrors. That'd shake her up.''

("I'm afraid not, Steve. You see, this creature is the source of the horrors.")

Dalt sat in stunned silence, then: "You always hinted that the horrors might be more than just a psychological disorder.''

("You must admit, I'm rarely wrong.")

"Yes, rarely wrong," Dalt replied tersely. "And frequently insufferable. But again: Why?''

("As I mentioned before, the human mind appears to be extraordinarily sensitive to her powers. She can reach across an entire galaxy and touch one of them. I believe she's been doing that for ages. At first she may only have been able to leave a vague impression. Long ago she was probably probing this arm of the galaxy and left an image within a fertile mind that started the murderous Kali cult in ancient India. Its members worshiped a many-armed goddess of death that bears a striking resemblance to our enemy. So for all practical purposes, we might as well call her Kali, since her given name is a mish-mash of consonants.")

"Whatever happened to the cult?''

("Died out. Perhaps she went back to concentrating on her own race, which was probably moving into space at about that time, and no doubt soon became busy with the task of annihilating the other races they encountered along the way.

("Then came a hiatus and her attention returned to us. Her powers had grown since last contact and although she was still unable to control a human mind, she found she could inundate it with such a flood of terror that the individual would withdraw completely from reality.")

"The horrors, in other words.''

("Right. She kept this up, biding her time until her race could devise a means of bridging the gap between the two races. They did. The apparatus occupies the space of a small town and is psionically activated. You know the rest of the story.")

"Yeah," Dalt replied, "and I can see what's coming, too. She's toying with us, isn't she? Playing a game of fear and terror, nibbling at us until we turn against each other. Humiliation, demoralization—they're dirty weapons."

("But not her final goal, I fear. Eventually she'll tire of the game and just wipe us out. And with ease! All she has to do is open the passage, slip through a short-timed planetary bomb, close the passage, and wait for the bang.")

"In two standard days," Dalt said in a shocked whisper, "she could destroy every inhabited planet in Occupied Space!"

("Probably wouldn't even take her that long. But we've quite a while to go before it comes to that. She's in no hurry. She'll probably chip away at us for a few centuries before delivering the coup de grace.") Pard went silent for a while. ("Which reminds me: I saw a major assault force gathered on the beach. If she really wanted to strike a demoralizing blow . . .")

"You don't think she'll hit Fed Central, do you?"

("With a second chance at interstellar unity almost within reach, can you think of a better target?")

"No, I can't," Dalt replied pensively. The thought of alien berserkers charging through the streets was not a pleasant one. "There must be a way to strike back."

("I'm sure there is. We just haven't thought of it yet. Sleep on it.")

Good idea. See you in the morning.

Morning brought Lenda with news that some of the flitter-probes were outfitted and ready. He invited Dalt to take a look at them. Lacking both the heart to tell Lenda that the probes were a futile gesture and anything better to do, he agreed to go along.

Arriving at a hanger atop one of the lesser buildings in the complex, he saw five drones completed and a sixth in the final stages. They looked like standard models except for the data-gathering instruments afixed to the hulls.

"They look like they've been sealed for pressurization," Dalt noted.

Lenda nodded. "Some of the sensors require it."

("I know what you're thinking!") Pard said.

Tell me.

("You want to equip these flitters with blaster cannon and attack Kali's island, don't you? Forget it! There are so many energy dampers in that temple that a blaster wouldn't even warm her skin if you could get near her. And you wouldn't. Her guards would cut you to ribbons.")

Maybe there's a way around that. He turned to Lenda. "Have Petrical meet me here. I have an errand to run but I'll be back shortly."

Lenda gave him a puzzled look as he walked away.

Dalt headed for the street. *Throw the Mordirak image around me. I don't want to be mobbed out there.*

("Done. Now tell me where we're going?")

Not far. He stepped outside and onto the local belt of the moving strol-lane. The streets were crowded. The new incoming representatives had brought their staffs and families and there were tourists constantly arriving to see the first General Council of the new Federation. He let the strol-lane carry him for a few minutes, then debarked before a blank-fronted store with only a simple handprinted sign over the door: WEAPONS.

Stepping through the filter field that screened the entrance, he was faced with an impressive array of death-dealing instruments. They gleamed from the racks and cases; they were sleek and sinister and beautiful and deadly.

"May I help you, sir?" asked a little man with squinty eyes.

"Where are your combustion weapons?"

"Ah!" he said, rubbing his palms together. "A sportsman or a collector?"

"Both."

"This way, please." He led them to the rear of the shop and placed himself behind a counter. "Now, then. Where does your interest lie? Handguns? Rifles? Shotguns? Automatics?"

"The last two."

"I beg your pardon?"

"I want an autoshotgun," Dalt said tersely. "Double-barreled with continuous feed."

"I'm afraid we only have one model along that line."

"I know. Ibizan makes it."

The man nodded and searched under the counter. He pulled out a shiny black case, placed it before him, and opened it.

Dalt inspected it briefly. "That's it. You have waist canisters for the feed?"

"Of course. The Ibizan is nonejecting, so you'll have to use disintegrating cases, you know."

"I know. Now. I want you to take this down to the workshop and cut the barrel off"—he drew a line with his finger—"right about here."

"Sir, you must be joking!" the little man said with visible shock, his eyes widening and losing their perpetual squint. But he could see by Dalt's expression that no joke was intended. He spoke petulantly. "I'm afraid I must see proof of credit before I deface such a fine weapon."

Dalt fished out a thin alloy disk and handed it over. The gunsmith pressed the disk into a notch in the counter and the image of Mordirak appeared in the hologram box beside it, accompanied by the number 1. Mordirak had first-class credit anywhere in Occupied Space.

With a sigh, the man handed back the disk, hefted the weapon, and took it into the enclosed workshop section.

("Your knowledge of weaponry is impressive.")

A holdover from my game-hunting days. Remember them?

("I remember disapproving of them.")

Well, combustion weapons are still in demand by "sportsmen" who find their sense of masculinity cheated by the lack of recoil in energy weapons.

("And just what is this Ibizan supposed to do for you?")

You'll see.

The gunsmith reappeared with the foreshortened weapon.

"You have a target range, I presume," Dalt said.

"Yes. On the lower level."

"Good. Fill the feeder with number-eight end-over-end cylindrical shot and we'll try her out."

The man winced but complied.

The target range was elaborate and currently set up with moving, bounding models of Kamedon deer. Sensors within the models rated the marksman's performance on a flashing screen at the firing line that could read "Miss," "Kill," "Wounded," and variations. The firing line was cleared as Dalt hooked the feed canister to his waist and fed the string of shells into the chambers. Flicking the safety off, he held the weapon against his chest with the barrels pointing downrange and began walking.

"Left barrel," he said, and pulled the trigger. The Ibizan jerked in his hands; the cannonlike roar was swallowed by the sound dampers but the muzzle flash was a good twenty centimeters in length, and one of the leaping targets was torn in half. "Right barrel," was faintly heard, with similar results. Then a flip of a switch and, "Automatic." The prolonged roar that issued from the rapidly alternating barrels taxed the sound dampers to their limit and when the noise stopped, every target hung in tatters. The indicator screen flashed solid red on and off in confusion.

"What could you possibly want to hunt with a weapon like that?" the little gunsmith asked, glancing from Dalt to the Ibizan to the ruined range.

A smug but irresistible reply came to mind.

"God."

"You wanted to see me about something?" Petrical asked.

"Yes. I have good reason to believe—please don't ask me why—that the next assault will be a big one and will be directed against Fed Central itself. I want you to out-fit these flitters with heavy-duty blasters and pick some of your best marksmen to man five of them. I'll take the sixth."

An amused expression crept over Petrical's face. "And just what do you plan to do with them?"

"We're going through the passage when it opens up," Dalt replied. "Maybe we can end these attacks once and for all."

Amusement was abruptly replaced by consternation. "Oh no, you're not! You're too valuable to risk on a suicide mission!"

"Unfortunately, I'm the only one who can do what must be done," Dalt said with a glare, "and since when do you dictate what I may and may not do."

But Petrical had been involved in too many verbal brawls on the floor of the General Council to be easily intimidated, even by The Healer. "I'll tell you what I *will* do, and that's have no part in helping you get your-self killed!"

"Mr. Petrical," Dalt said in a low voice, "do I have to outfit my own flitter and go through alone?"

Petrical opened his mouth for a quick reply and then closed it. He knew when he was outflanked. With the new General Council arriving for the emergency session, all that was needed to bring the walls tumbling down upon his head was news that he had let The Healer take the war to the enemy alone—with no backup from the Federation Defense Force.

"But the probes were your idea. . . ."

"The probes have been rendered obsolete by new in-formation. The only solution is to go through."

"Well then, let me send a bigger force."

"No." Dalt shook his head. "If these six flitters can't do the job, then six hundred wouldn't make any dif-ference."

"All right." Petrical grunted with exasperation. "I'll

get the armorers down here and start asking for volunteers.''

Dalt's smile was genuine. "Thanks. And don't delay—we may not have much time. Oh, and have an alarm system set up here in the hangar to notify us the minute a vortex is sighted. We'll live in and around the flitters until the attack comes. I'll brief your men on what to expect and what to do.''

Petrical nodded with obvious reluctance.

("Why haven't I been consulted on any of this?'') Pard asked indignantly as Dalt returned to his quarters.

Because I already know your answer.

("I'm sure you do. It's all insanity and I want no part of it!'')

You don't have much choice.

("Be reasonable!'')

Pard, this is something we must do.

("Why?'') The voice in his head was angry. ("To live up to your legend?'')

In a way, yes. You and I are the only ones who can beat her.

("You're sure of that?'')

Aren't you? Pard did not reply and Dalt felt a sudden chill. *Answer me: Are you afraid of this Kali creature?*

("Yes.'')

Why should you be? You defeated her at every turn when we were battling the horrors.

("That was different. There was no direct contact there. We were merely fighting the residue of her influence, a sort of resonating circuit of afterimages. We've only come into direct contact with her once . . . on the beach on Clutch. And you know what happened there.'')

Yeah, Dalt replied slowly. *We were blasted apart.*

("Exactly. This creature's psi powers are immense. She's keyed her whole existence toward developing them because her dominion over her race springs from them. I estimate she had a four-thousand-year head start on

us. All the defense precautions around her island temple
—the energy dampers, the guards with their ridiculous
costumes and ancient weapons—would not stand up
against a single mercenary soldier in regulation battle
gear. They're trappings required by her paranoia. The
real defense system of that temple is in her mind. She
can psionically fry any brain in her star system that
threatens her. Short of an automated Federation dreadnaught turning her entire planet to ash—and we have no
way of getting one within half a galaxy of her—she's
virtually impregnable.")

Pard paused for effect, then: ("You still want to go
after her?")

Dalt hesitated, but only briefly. *Yes.*

("Insanity!") Pard exploded. ("Sheer, undiluted,
raving insanity! Usually I can follow your reasoning,
but this is one big blur. Is there some sort of racial urge
involved? Do you feel you owe it to humanity to go
down fighting? Is this a noble gesture or what?")

I don't know, exactly.

("You're right, you don't know! You owe your race
nothing! You've given it far more than it's given you.
Your primary responsibility is to yourself. Sacrificing
your—*our*—life is a meaningless gesture!")

*It's not meaningless. And if we succeed, it won't be a
sacrifice.*

("We have about as much chance of defeating her as
we have of growing flowers on a neutron star. I forbid
it!")

You can't. You owe it.

("To whom?")

*To me. This is my life and my body. You've aug-
mented it, improved it, and extended it, true, but you've
shared equally in the benefits. It remains my life and
you've shared it. I'm asking for an accounting.*

Pard waited a long time before giving his reply.
("Very well, then. We'll go.") There was a definite edge
on the thought. ("But neither of us should make any
long-range plans.")

•   •   •

With the flitters armed, the volunteers briefed, and the practice runs made, Dalt and his crew settled down for an uneasy vigil.

Think we'll have a long wait? Dalt asked.

("I doubt it. The Kalians looked almost set to go when I saw them.")

Well, at least we'll get enough sleep. If there's been any consistency at all in the attacks, it's been their occurrence in daylight hours.

("That may not be the case this time. If my guess is right and they are aiming for Fed Central, their tactics might be different. For all we know, they may just want to set up a device to destroy the Federation Complex.")

Dalt groaned softly. *That would be a crippling coup.*

("Nonsense! The Federation is more than a few buildings. It's a concept . . . an idea.")

It's also an organization; and if there's one thing we need now, it's organization. There's a nucleus of a new Federation growing over at the General Council at this moment. Destroy that and organized resistance will be completely unraveled.

("Perhaps not.")

The Kalians are united wholeheartedly behind their goddess. Who've we got?

("The Healer, of course.")

At this point, if the Federation Complex is destroyed, so is The Healer. Dalt glanced up at the alarm terminal with its howlers and flashers ready to go. *I just hope that thing goes off in time for us to get through the passage.*

("If it goes off, it will probably do so because you set it off.")

What's that supposed to mean?

("The passage is psionically activated and directed by Kali, remember? If a psi force of that magnitude appears anywhere on Fed Central, I'll know about it—immediately.")

"Oh," Dalt muttered aloud. "Well, let's hope it's soon, then. This waiting is nerve-wracking."

("I'll be quite happy if they never show up.")

"We've already been through that!"

"Pardon me, sir," said a trooper passing within ear-shot.

"What is it?" Dalt asked.

The trooper looked flustered. "I thought you spoke to me."

"Huh? Oh, no." Dalt smiled weakly. "Just thinking out loud."

"Yessir." He nodded and walked on by with a quick backward glance.

("He thinks you may be crazy,") Pard needled. ("So do I, but for entirely different reasons.")

Quiet and let me sleep.

Their vigil was not a long one. Before dawn on the second day, Dalt suddenly found himself wide awake, his sympathetic nervous system vibrating with alarm.

("Hit the button,") Pard said reluctantly. ("They're here.")

Where?

("About two kilometers away. I'll lead everyone there.")

Fastening the Ibizan feeder belt to his waist as he ran, Dalt activated the alarm and the twenty marksmen were blared and strobed to wakefulness.

The sergeant in charge of the detail trotted up to Dalt. "Where we going?"

Dalt withheld a shrug and said, "Just follow me."

With the activation of the alarm, the hangar roof irised open and the six armed and pressurized flitters were airborne in less than a minute. Pard guided Dalt high above the Federation Complex.

("Now drop and bank off to the left of that building that looks like an inverted pyramid.")

"That's where they are?" Dalt exclaimed.

("Yes. Right in the heart of the complex.")

"From tens of thousands of light-years away . . . how can they be so accurate?"

("Not 'they'—*she*. Kali directs the passage.")

With their running lights out, the flitters sank between two smooth-walled buildings until they hovered only a few meters above the pavement.

("It's at the far end of the alley.")

Dalt shook his heading in grudging respect. "Pinpoint accuracy."

("And strategically brilliant. There's almost no room to maneuver against them here. I warned you she was a formidable opponent—still want to go through with this?")

Dalt wished he could frame a recklessly courageous reply but none was forthcoming. Instead, he activated the search beams on the front of the flitter and illuminated a chilling sight: The invaders were pouring from their hole in space like angry insects from a hive.

As the flitters came under immediate fire, Dalt gunned his craft to full throttle and it leaped ahead on a collision course with the oncoming horde. Invaders were knocked over or butted aside as he rammed into them. He noted that the flitters behind him were returning fire as they ran—

—and then all was gray, toneless, flat and silent as they passed through the vortex and into subspace. Dalt felt a brief rush of vertigo as he lost his horizon in the featureless void but managed to hold a steady course past surprised and wildly gesticulating invaders on their way to Fed Central.

("Keep her steady for just a little longer and we'll be there.")

Pard had no sooner given this encouragement than the craft burst into sunlight, bowling over more invaders in the process. Without a backward glance, Dalt kept the throttle at full and pulled for altitude toward the sea.

("See the island?")

"Straight ahead."

("Right. Keep going.")

"I just hope the sergeant remembered to tell Petrical where the breakthrough was before he went through."

("Don't worry about that. The sergeant's a seasoned trooper. We've got bigger problems ahead.")

The following flitters were through now and were busily engaged in strafing the Kalian encampments on the shore. Their mission was to cripple the attack on Fed Central and prevent any countermove against Dalt as he headed for the island.

("Veer toward the south side,") Pard told him.

"Which way is south?"

("Left.")

They were near enough now to make out gross details of the temple.

"Where do I land?"

("You don't. At least not yet. See that large opening there? Fly right into it.")

"Doesn't look very big."

("If you could thread that vortex, you can thread that corridor.")

The guardians of the fortress-temple were waiting for them at the entrance with arrows nocked, bows drawn, and spears at the ready.

("Slow up and hit them with the blasters,") Pard directed.

That seemed too brutal to Dalt. "I'll just ride right through them. They're only armed with sharpened sticks."

("I'll remind you of that when they swarm over us from behind and spit your body like a piece of meat. Compassion dulls your memory. Have you forgotten the bathers on Clutch? Or that little boy?")

Enough! Dalt filled his lungs and pressed the newly installed weapons button on the console. The blasters hummed but the guards remained undaunted and uninjured.

"What's wrong?"

("Nothing, except the energy dampers are more powerful than I expected. We may not even get near Kali.")

"Oh, we'll get there, all right." Dalt gunned his craft to top speed again as he dropped the keel to a half meter above the stone steps. Spears and arrows clattered ineffectively off the hull and enclosed cabin but the guards held their ground until Dalt was almost upon them.

Then they broke formation. The quick dove for the sides and most escaped unharmed. The slower ones were hurled in all directions by the prow of the onrushing craft.

Then darkness. At Pard's prompting, Dalt's pupils dilated immediately to full aperture and details were suddenly visible in the dimly lit corridor. The historical frescoes Pard had seen on his previous visit blurred by on either side. Ahead, the corridor funneled down to a low narrow archway.

"I don't think I can make that," Dalt said.

("I don't think so, either. But you can probably use it to hamper pursuit a bit.")

"I was thinking the same thing." He abruptly slowed the craft and let it glide into the opening until both sides crunched against stone. "That oughta do it." The side hatch was flush against the side of the arch, so he broke pressure by lowering the foreward windshield. Cool, damp, musty air filtered into the cabin, carrying a tang of salt and a touch of mildew.

He fed the first round from the canister into the sawed-off Ibizan and climbed out onto the deck. As he slid to the floor, something clattered against the hull close by and an instant later he felt an impact and a grating pain in the right side of his back. Spinning on his heel, he sensed something whiz over his head as he flipped the Ibizan to auto and fired a short burst in an arc.

Four Kalians in a doorway to his right were spun and thrown around by the ferocious spray of shot, then lay still.

What hit me? The pain was gone from his back.

("An arrow. It glanced off the eighth rib on the right and is now imbedded in the intercostal muscle. A poor shot—hit you on an angle and didn't make it through the pleura. I've put a sensory block on the area.")

Good. Which way now?

("Through that doorway. And hurry!")

As Dalt crossed the threshold into a small chamber, another arrow caught him in the left thigh. Again, he opened up the Ibizan and sprayed the room. He took a few of his own ricocheting pellets in the chest, but the seven Kalians lying in wait for him had taken most of them.

("Keep going!") There was more than a trace of urgency in the directive.

He managed to run, although his left leg dragged somewhat due to the arrow's mechanical impediment of muscle action. But he felt no pain from this wound either. As he left the bloody anteroom and entered another corridor, his vision suddenly blurred and his equilibrium wavered.

What was that?

("The same knockout punch that separated us on Clutch. Only this time I was ready for it. Now the going gets tough—the lady has decided to step in.")

Dalt started to run forward again but glanced down and found himself at the edge of a yawning pit. Something large and hungry thrashed and splashed in the inky darkness below.

"Where'd that come from?" he whispered hoarsely.

("From Kali's mind. It's not real—keep going.")

You sure?

("Positive . . . I think.")

Oh, great! Dalt gritted his teeth and began to run. To his immense relief, his feet struck solid ground, even though he seemed to be running on air.

White tentacles, slime-coated and as thick as his thighs, sprang out from the walls and reached for him. He halted again.

Same thing?

("I hope so. You're only seeing a small fraction of what I'm seeing. I'm screening most of it. And so far she's only toying with us. I'll bet she's holding back until—")

A spear scaled off the wall to his right, forestalling further discussion. As Dalt turned with the Ibizan at the ready, an arrow plunged into the fleshy fossa below his left clavicle. The guards from the entrance to the temple had found a way around the flitter and were now charging down the corridor in pursuit. With a flash that lit up the area and a roar that was deafening in those narrow confines, the Ibizan scythed through the onrushing ranks, leaving many dead and the rest disabled, but not before Dalt had taken another arrow below the right costal margin. Fluid that looked to be a mixture of green, yellow, and red began to drip along the shaft.

How many of these things can I take? I'm beginning to look like a Neekan spine worm!

("A lot more. But not too many more like that last one. It pierced the hepatic duct and you're losing bile. Blood, too. I can't do too much to control the bleeding from the venous sinusoids in the liver. But we'll be all right as long as no arrows lodge in any of the larger joints or sever a major motor axon bundle, either of which would severely hamper mobility. The one under your clavicle was a close call; just missed the brachial plexus. Another centimeter higher and you'd have lost the use of your . . .")

The words seemed to fade out.

"Pard?" Dalt said.

(". . . run!") The thought was strained, taut. ("She's hitting us with everything now. . . .") Fade out again. Then, ("I'll tell you where to turn!")

Dalt ran with all the speed he could muster, limping with his left leg and studiously trying to avoid contact between the narrow walls and the shafts protruding from his body. The corridor became a maze with turns every few meters. At each intersection he would hear a faint ("left") or ("right") in his mind. And as minutes passed, the voice became progressively weaker until it was barely distinguishable among his own thoughts.

("Please hurry!") Pard urged faintly and Dalt realized that he must be taking a terrible beating—in twelve hundred years Pard had never said "please."

("Two more left turns and you're there . . . don't hesitate . . . start firing as soon as you make the last turn. . . .")

Dalt nodded in the murk and double-checked the automatic setting, fully intending to do just that. But when the moment came, when he made the final turn, he hesitated for a heartbeat, just long enough to see what he would be shooting at.

She lay there, propped up on cushions and smiling at him. El. Somehow it didn't seem at all incongruous that she should be there. Her death nearly a millennium ago had all been a bad dream. But he had awakened now and this was Tolive, not some insane planet on the far side of the galaxy.

He stepped toward her and was about to let the Ibizan slip from his fingers when every neuron in his body was jolted with a single message:

"Fire!"

His finger tightened on the trigger reflexively and El exploded in a shower of red. He was suddenly back in reality and he held the roaring, swerving, bucking weapon on target until the feed canister was empty.

The echoes faded, and finally, silence.

There was not too much left of Kali. Dalt only glanced at the remains, turned, and retched. As he gasped for air and wiped clammy beads of sweat from his upper lip, he asked Pard, *No chance of regeneration, is there?*

No answer.

"Pard?" he called aloud, and underwent an alarming instant of déjà vu. But this time he knew Pard was still there—an indefinable sense signaled his presence. Pard was injured, weakened, scarred, and had retreated to a far corner of Dalt's brain. But he was still there.

Without daring a backward glance, he tucked the Ibizan into the crook of his right arm, its barrel aligned with the arrow protruding from his liver, and reentered the maze. He was concerned at first with finding his way out, until he noticed drops of a familiar muddy fluid on the floor in the dim light. He had left a trail of blood and bile as it oozed from his liver, along the arrow shaft and onto the floor.

With only a few wrong turns, he managed to extricate himself from the maze and limp back to the flitter. There he was confronted with another problem.

A large group of Kali's guards stood clustered around the craft. Dalt's immediate reaction was to shift the Ibizan and reach for the trigger. A gesture as futile as it was unnecessary: the weapon was empty, and at sight of him, the guards threw down their arms and prostrated themselves face down on the ground before him.

They know she's dead, he thought. *Somehow, they know.* He hesitated only a moment, then stepped gingerly between the worshipers and their dead brethren who had attacked him earlier.

He had a difficult moment entering the flitter when the arrows protruding from the front and back of his chest caught on the window opening. The problem was resolved when he snapped off the shaft of the arrow under the clavicle a handsbreadth away from his skin.

Situating himself again at the console, he first replaced the empty feeder canister with a fresh one—just in case—and activated the instruments before him. The vid screen to his right immediately lit up with the sergeant's face. Dalt made a quick adjustment of the transmitting lens to limit focus to his face.

"Healer!" the sergeant exclaimed with obvious relief. "You're all right?"

"Fine," Dalt replied. "How are things over there?"

The sergeant grinned. "It was rough going for a while—couple of the flitters took a beating and one's down. But just when things were starting to look really bad, the opposition folded . . . just threw down their weapons and went into fits on the beach . . . ignored us completely. Some of them dove into the ocean and started swimming toward the island. The rest are just moping aimlessly along the water's edge."

"Everything's secure, then?" Dalt asked. The flitter's engine was humming now. He pulled the guide stick into reverse and upped the power. The craft vibrated as it tried to disengage from the doorway. With a grating

screech, the flitter came free and caromed off the port
wall before Dalt could throttle down and stabilize. The
corridor was too narrow here to make a full turn, so
he resigned himself to gliding part of the way out in
reverse.

The sergeant said something but Dalt missed it and
asked him to repeat. "I said, there's a couple of my men
burned but they should do all right if we get back."

With his head turned over his left shoulder and two
fingers on the guide stick, Dalt was concentrating fully
on piloting the flitter in reverse. It was not until he
reached the point where the corridor widened to its
fullest expanse that the "if" broke through.

"What do you mean, 'if'?" he asked, throwing the
gears into neutral and hitting the button that would
automatically guide the flitter in a 180-degree turn on its
own axis.

"The gate or passage or warp or whatever you want
to call it—it's closed," he replied. "How're we going to
get home?"

Dalt felt a tightness in his throat but put on a brave
face. "Just sit tight till I get there. Out."

"Right," the sergeant said, instantly reassured. He
was convinced The Healer could do anything. "Out."
The vid plate went black.

Dalt put the problem of crossing the sixty thousand
light-years that separated his little group from the rest
of humanity out of his mind and concentrated on the
patch of light ahead of him. The return had been too
easy so far. He could not help but expect some sort of
reprisal, and his head pivoted continuously as he gained
momentum toward the end of the corridor and daylight.

But no countermove was in the offing. As Dalt shot
from the darkness into the open air, he saw the steps
leading to the temple entrance blanketed with prostrate
Kalians. Most eyes stayed earthward, but here and there
a head was raised as he soared over the crowd and
headed for the mainland. He could not read individual
expressions but there was a terrible sense of loss in their

postures and movements. The ones who looked after him seemed to be saying, "You've killed our godhead and now disdain to take her place, leaving us with nothing."

Dalt felt sudden pity for the Kalians. Their entire culture had been twisted, corrupted, and debased by a single being. And now that being was no more. Utter chaos would follow. But from the rubble would rise a new, broader-based society, hopefully with a more benign god, or perhaps no god. Anything would be an improvement.

("Perhaps,") said a familiar voice, ("their new god will be Kalianoid with a white patch of hair and a golden hand. And minstrels will sing of how he crossed the void, shrugged off their arrows and spears, and went on to overpower the all-powerful, to slay She-Who-Could-Not-Die.")

Gained your strength back, I see.

("Not quite. I may never fully recover from that ordeal. All debts are paid, I hope, because I will never risk my existence like that again.")

I sincerely hope such a situation will never arise again. And yes, all debts are paid in full.

("Good. And if you awaken in the middle of the night now and again with the sound of horrified screaming in your brain, don't worry. It'll be me remembering what I've just been through.")

That bad, eh?

("I'm amazed we survived—and that's all I'll say on the matter.")

Details of the coast were coming into view now, and below, Dalt spotted an occasional Kalian swimming desperately for the island.

You know about the warp generator? Dalt asked.

("Yes. As I told you before, Kali activated it psionically. She's dead now so it's quite logical that it should cease to function. I think I can activate it briefly. So call the sergeant and have him get his men into the air—we'll have to make this quick.")

Dalt did so, and found four of the five flitters, each overloaded with men from the disabled craft, hovering over the shore.

("Here goes,") Pard said. ("I can only hope that there was some sort of lock on the settings, because I haven't the faintest idea how to direct the passage. We could end up in the middle of a sun or somewhere off the galactic rim.")

Dalt said only, "Do it!" and pressurized the cabin.

Nothing happened for a while, then a gray disk appeared. It expanded gradually, evenly, and as soon as its diameter appeared sufficient to accommodate a flitter, Dalt threw the stick forward and plunged into the unknown.

XXII

THEY SEEMED TO drift in the two-dimensional grayness interminably. Then, as if passing through a curtain, they were in real space, in daylight, on Fed Central. And what appeared to be the entire Federation Defense Force clogged the alley before them and the air above them in full battle readiness. There was more lethal weaponry crammed into that little alley than was contained on many an entire planet. And it was all trained on Dalt.

Ever so gently, he guided his flitter to ground between incinerated Kalian bodies and sat quietly, waiting for the following craft to do the same. When the last came through, the vortex collapsed upon itself and disappeared.

("That's the end of that!") Pard said with relief. ("Unless the Kalian race develops another psi freak who can learn to operate it, the warp passage will never open again.")

Good. By the time we run into them again—a few millennia hence, no doubt—they should be quite a bit more tractable.

With the closing of the passage, the marksmen in the other craft opened all the hatches and tumbled out to the pavement. At the sight of their comrades, the battle-ready troops around them lowered their weapons and pandemonium broke out. The flitters were suddenly surrounded by cheering, waving soldiers.

Ros Petrical seemed to appear out of nowhere, riding a small, open grav platform. The milling troops made way for him as he landed beside Dalt's flitter.

Dalt opened the hatch and came out to meet him. His effect on the crowd was immediate. As his head appeared and the snowy patch of hair was recognized, a loud cheer arose; but when his body came into view, the cheer choked and died. There followed dead silence broken only by occasional murmurs of alarm.

"Pardon my appearance," Dalt said, glancing at the bloody shafts protruding from his body and tucking the Ibizan under his arm, "but I ran into a little resistance."

Petrical swallowed hard. "You really are The Healer!" he muttered.

"You mean to say you had your doubts?" Dalt asked with a wry smile as he stepped onto the platform.

Petrical shot the platform above the silent crowd. "Frankly, yes. I've always thought there was a chain of Healers . . . but I guess you're the real thing."

"Guess so. Where're we going?"

"Well, I had planned to take you to the Council session; they're waiting to hear from you in person." He glanced at the arrows. "But that can wait. I'm taking you to the infirmary."

Dalt laid a hand on his arm. "To the Council. I'm quite all right. After all," he said, quoting a line that was centuries old, " 'what kind of a healer would The Healer be if he couldn't heal himself?' "

Petrical shook his head in bafflement and banked toward the General Council hall.

A sequence of events similar to that which had occurred in the alley was repeated in the Council hall. The delegates and representatives had received word that The Healer's mission had been successful and that he was on his way to address them personally. Many of the men and women in the chamber were members of The Healer cult and started cheering and chanting before he appeared. As in the alley, a great shout went up at first sight of him on the high dais, but this was instantly snuffed out when it became obvious that he was mortally wounded. But Dalt waved and smiled to reassure them and then the uproar resumed with renewed intensity.

Between horrified glances at Dalt's punctured body, the elderly president pro tem of the Council was trying to bring order to the meeting and was being completely ignored. The delegates and reps were in the aisles, shouting, waving, and hugging one another. Dalt spotted Lenda standing quietly amid the Clutch delegation. Their eyes met and Dalt nodded his congratulations. The nod was returned with a smile.

After a few minutes of the tumult, Dalt began to grow impatient. Switching the Ibizan to the single-shot mode, he handed it to the president pro tem.

"Use this as a gavel."

The old man took it with a knowing grin and aimed the weapon at the high ceiling. He let off four rounds in rapid succession. The acoustic material above absorbed the end-over-end shot with ease but was less successful in handling the accompanying roar. The crowd quieted abruptly.

"Now that I have your attention," he said with forced sternness, "please take your places."

The Council members laughed good-naturedly and complied.

"I've never seen or heard of a more vigorous, more vital, more rowdy bunch of representatives in my life!" Petrical whispered, his face flushed with excitement.

Dalt nodded and inwardly told Pard, *I feel pretty vigorous myself.*

("About time,") came the sardonic reply. ("It's been a couple of centuries since you've shown much life.")

The president pro tem was speaking. "We have before us a motion to install The Healer as chief executive of the Federation by acclaim. Now what I propose to do is . . ." Even with amplification at maximum, his voice was lost in the joyous chaos that was unleashed by the announcement.

Shrugging, the old man stepped back from the podium and decided to let the demonstration run its course. The pandemonium gradually took the form of a chant.

". . . HEALER! HEALER! HEALER! . . ."

Pard became a demon voice in Dalt's mind. ("They're in the palm of your hand. Take command and you can direct the course of human history from now on.")

And be another Kali?

("Your influence wouldn't have to be malevolent. Look at them! Tarks, Lentemians, Humans! Think of all the great things you could lead them to!")

Dalt considered this as he watched the crowd and drank in its intoxicating chant:

". . . HEALER! HEALER! HEALER! . . ."

Thoughts of Tolive suddenly flashed before him. *You know my answer!*

("You're not even tempted?")

Not in the least. I can't remember when I last felt so alive, and I find there are many things I still want to do, many goals I still want to achieve. Power isn't one of them.

Pard's silence indicated approval. ("What will you tell them?") he asked finally.

Don't know, exactly. Something about holding to the LaNague charter, about letting the Federation be the focus of their goals but never allowing those goals to originate here. Peace, freedom, love, friendship, happiness, prosperity, and other sundry political catchwords. But the big message will be a firm "No thanks!"

("You're sure now?") Pard taunted. ("You don't want to be acclaimed leader of the entire human race and a few others as well?")

I've got better things to do.

EPILOGUE

Kolko lounged by the fire and eyed the wagon that sat in darkness on the far side of the flames. His troupe of Thespelian gypsies had turned in early tonight in preparation for their arrival in Lanthus tomorrow. Kolko was hurt and angry—but only a little. Thalana had taken up with the new mentalist and wanted no part of him.

He was tempted to enter the darkened wagon and confront the two of them but had decided against it for a number of reasons. First off, he had no real emotional attachment to Thalana, nor she to him. His pride was in pain, not his heart. Secondly, a row over a love triangle would only cause needless dissension in the peaceful little company. And finally, it would mean facing up to the new mentalist, a thought he did not relish.

An imposing figure, this newest member of the troupe, with all of his skin dyed gold and his hair dyed silver . . . a melding of precious metals. And quite a talent. Kolko had seen mentalists come and go but could not figure out how this one pulled off his stunts.

A likable fellow, but distant. Hiding from his past, no doubt, but that hardly made him unique among the gypsies of Thespel. He would laugh with the group around the fire and could drink an incredible amount of wine without ever opening up. Always one step removed. And he had an odd habit of muttering to himself now and again, but nobody ever mentioned it to him . . . there was an air about the man that brooked no meddling with his personal affairs or habits.

So let him have Thalana. There would be other dancers joining the troupe along the way, probably better-looking than Thalana and better in the bedroll . . . although that would take some doing.

Let 'em be. Life was too good these days. Good wine, good company, good weather, good crowds of free-spending people in the towns.

He picked up an arthritic tree limb and stirred the coals, watching the sparks swirl gently upward to mingle with the pinpoint stars overhead.

Let 'em be.